Gillian Leggat is a prolific author of more than sixty books. She has been published in various genres including young adult novels, text books, readers, and picture books. She has a Masters degree in English and has taught at a variety of schools and colleges. Currently, she tutors English, runs writing classes and trains adults. She is widowed and has three adult children and one grandchild. She lives in Cape Town where, surrounded by natural beauty and inspired by excellent teaching at her church, she is motivated to write more books.

HEADLINES IN HEAVEN

Gillian Leggat

HEADLINES IN HEAVEN

Vanguard Press

A CIP catalogue record for this title is
available from the British Library.

ISBN 978 178465 259 3

*Vanguard Press is an imprint of
Pegasus Elliot MacKenzie Publishers Ltd.*
www.pegasuspublishers.com

First Published in 2017

Vanguard Press
Sheraton House Castle Park
Cambridge England

Printed & Bound in Great Britain

For Jennie, Robert and Susan

Chapter One

Raphael had just winged his way to the open court in front of the throne room. One of his favourite duties was to meet the new saints and usher them into the very presence of the King himself. Every time he saw the sheer delight and amazement on their faces as he led them across the marble floor, around the crystal fountain and through the massive, bejewelled pillars, he experienced a fresh surge of joy. And when he flew with them into the throne room itself, his joy turned to ecstasy.

Before he even guided them through the perfect archway, his ears were assailed with the rich, melodious voices of thousands upon thousands of angelic choristers lifting their perfectly-tuned voices to praise their Almighty Lord, the Maker and King of the universe. It gladdened his heart to watch the effect of these exquisite harmonies on each group of novice saints, especially on the children. In fact, the younger they arrived in the kingdom, the more uninhibited they were. The older saints tended to drop to their knees in worship; not so the younger ones. They wanted to sing and dance, clap and stamp, celebrating by using every inch of their vibrant young bodies – so exciting to watch.

But the minute they stepped through the archway into the very throne room of the Lord himself, even the young saints collapsed onto their knees, some of them prostrating themselves on the kaleidoscopic floor. As the angel choirs sang "Holy, holy, holy is the Lord God Almighty, who was, and is, and is to come", (Revelation 4 v 8), all the new arrivals were understandably completely overwhelmed by the beauty and majesty and glory and power of our Almighty God. They lay, kneeled, bowed down, hid their faces; but as with many of the other groups Raphael had welcomed into the kingdom, this bunch had fallen completely silent in awe.

Even though it was so long ago, at the dawn of time, he remembered that magnificent moment when he had stood at the threshold of God's throne room for the first time. The Lord himself was so glorious and so bright that he had the appearance of jasper and carnelian. And then there was a rainbow, which looked like an emerald, encircling the throne. And God's wasn't the only throne: in amazement, he had counted twenty-four other thrones, filled with elders dressed in white, with crowns of gold on their heads. In front of God's throne, there were seven lamps, which he learnt later were representative of the seven spirits of God. And so shimmering was the area directly in front of the throne – clear as crystal, like a sea of glass, that Raphael had to shield his eyes for a while until he got used to the brilliant light. The four living, eye-covered, multiple-winged creatures surrounding the throne, at the very heart of all that luminous light, constantly worshipped the Lord. So sight wasn't the only sense that was bedazzled: apart from the flashes of lightning coming directly from the Lord's throne being accompanied by loud rumblings and peals of thunder, the rich melodious voices of these four creatures – who looked like a lion, an ox, a man and a flying eagle – filled the throne room with sublime harmonies as they sang "Holy, holy, holy is the Lord God Almighty, who was, and is, and is to come."(Revelation 4 v 8) The elders' awed response was delivered from a lowly position, as they fell down and worshipped the Lord God Almighty as they sang "You are worthy, our Lord and God, to receive glory and honour and power, for you created all things, and by your will they were created and have their being." (Revelation 4 v 11)

Looking now at the silent group of saints who lay prostrate on the shining floor in front of their Lord and Master, Raphael wasn't surprised by their attitude. Who would be able to resist a posture of humble worship when presented with the glorious King of the Universe?

However, he was surprised when the Son of God, Jesus Christ himself, left his place at his Father's side and walked purposefully right into their midst. "Get up, my children. Rise, my brothers, my sisters, my mothers. Welcome to the kingdom of heaven." He paused, looking reflective, then continued: "I will be leaving you for a while – for thirty-three earth years – but you will be very well looked after in my Father's wonderful land. Don't be afraid of him: he is mighty indeed, and powerful and holy… but unless I go to the place you have just come from, there will be a drastic decline in the number of saints entering the kingdom." He turned away rather sadly, looking towards his Father.

"My son, my beloved son," said the Lord and Master, the Almighty Creator of the whole universe.

"My Father."

No further words were necessary. The intensity of the look they exchanged was shimmeringly bright, more glowing than the glistening lights emanating from the jasper, gold, sapphire, chalcedony, emerald, sardonyx, carnelian, chrysolite, beryl, topaz, chrysoprase, jacinth, amethyst or pearl that shone in the throne room itself. (Revelation 21 vs 18-21)

Raphael was still reflecting on the meaning of this heartfelt exchange between the Father and his beloved Son when he heard an urgent trumpet-call. Michael, one of the archangels, was summoning him to his next duty. Someone else would be assigned the task of familiarising this fresh family with their brand new home.

Instantaneously, Raphael lifted his wings, speeding to Michael's luxuriant garden. As soon as he arrived, the angel at his side who was acting as his messenger lowered his trumpet. Michael indicated that he should sit opposite him on the smooth marble bench under the wide-spreading branches of the oldest oak tree in the garden. Immediately he obliged, waiting deferentially for the command of his superior.

"I have summoned you from the throne room on an important mission, Raphael."

"I will serve the Lord with gladness," he replied.

"What I am about to ask of you will not be easy," warned Michael.

"I'm not a fighter, Michael," he replied with trepidation, his mind flashing back to the great battle preceding the moment that Satan was flung from the kingdom. "But if the Lord needs me in battle, I will go willingly into the fray."

"You are, indeed, required to go into the fray, but not in the way you are expecting. The only weapon you will be using is" – he paused dramatically – "the mighty pen."

"The pen… ?"

"The very same. It has come to our Lord and Master's attention that you are good with words. He needs a chronicler… if you were a man on earth, you would be called a reporter."

"A reporter? You mean a messenger?"

"Yes and no. You will certainly be delivering messages to the angels and saints in our heavenly kingdom, but you will be doing more than that."

"Am I to go to earth then?"

"Yes. But as a reporter, not a messenger. You will be following the events that unfold in a certain country called Israel..."

"The promised land."

"Yes. But you will be paying particular attention to what goes on in the towns of Bethlehem, Nazareth, Capernaum, Jericho, Jerusalem… "

"For what purpose?"

"Because the angels and saints in heaven need to know what is going on down there on earth during this crucial period of the world's history," replied Michael. "You will be writing up events in *The Heavenly Chronicle.*

"How exciting," he said suddenly. "I'm an angel of words, not wars. What a privilege to be tasked with such a responsible mission."

"But you do need to know that because of the complexity of the task and your expertise in the area, you will be the sole reporter/editor/proof-reader. Due to the onerousness of the task, you will, for a time, be relieved of all your other heavenly duties."

"How long is 'for a time'?"

"For thirty-three earth years." Michael's reply was solemn, almost sad. "But you will not need to report for the whole duration: just the initial miracle and one important event soon after that, then there will be a gap of thirty years before you begin reporting on the ministry itself."

"And then just three after that? What will I be doing during the thirty years in between?"

"Watching – and waiting. Observing – and learning. Especially picking up background detail about specific places."

"I can do that!" he smiled.

"You'll be learning a great deal."

"And how will I know when my waiting period is over?"

"Oh, you will know."

"It will be that obvious?"

"It certainly will. Trust me. Now. Your mission will begin in exactly nine months' time, and you have a great deal of preparation to do. Headlines. Topic sentences. First paragraphs, especially the who, what, where, when and why rules that are basic to all journalists on earth. Practice makes perfect, and *The Heavenly Chronicle* needs to be perfect: the very best it can be. There will be many spirits in the heavenly realms who will be learning about what is happening on earth from your articles. So don't waste any time: get to work as soon as possible."

"May I ask one question?"

"You may."

"Why thirty years? Why a couple of initial reports – then a gap? Why three years only after that? I'm confused."

"The secrets of the kingdom will be revealed in due course. They will unfold in front of your very eyes and you will record the events on earth faithfully for the spirits in the heavenly realms. Now go. There is important work to be done."

Raphael wouldn't have dreamt of questioning his superior further, but he did feel slightly frustrated that he was going into this job in the dark. An intelligent angel, he liked to know the reason for things: blind faith and trust were difficult for him, but he knew duty, so he winged off instantly to begin his task. As he was flying through the heavens, he did experience a sudden flashback to the earnest exchange between the Father and the Son only a short while ago in the throne room. Thirty-three years. The Son leaving the Father. To go to the Earth? Why would he do that?

It was unthinkable for the very creator and sustainer of the universe to leave his brilliant home in the heavens for that tiny speck of matter light years away from the elevated place he enjoyed at his Father's side. How would the Father and Son survive without being able to commune constantly with each other? And how would the perfect, spotless Christ be able to tolerate living amongst those wicked men and women in the devil's thrall?

And he, Raphael, was the angel assigned to reporting on thirty-three years of sacrifice that his Lord and Master, Christ the King, was about to undertake! He only hoped he was up to the task, and that he would be able to report accurately and fairly the events that were about to unfold on the earth.

So began his months of preparation. He meticulously recorded what was going on in the heavenly realms, starting with himself and his immediate circle of angels. As Michael had advised, he practised headlines, topic sentences, the who, what, where, when and why rule that was so important for a good article. He tried to make his prose interesting and readable. He experimented with his use of syntax: sometimes placing the most important information at the beginning of the sentence or paragraph, and sometimes placing it at the end. He tested his skill of building up to a climax. As a contrast, he occasionally used anti-climax. He edited his work, crossing out, replacing, inserting, on a constant mission to improve his standard of writing for the important mission that had been assigned to him. He put in a great number of hours during each heavenly cycle to get his style right. He even missed some of the praise sessions in the throne room – which he regretted afterwards, deciding that they would have inspired him a great deal; and if he was going to make his pen powerful, he would need all the inspiration he could get.

When the time drew near for his actual task to begin, instead of feeling elated, he found that he was extremely nervous, not trusting in his own ability. He really didn't feel he was the best angel for the job. But Michael reminded him that it was the Lord's strength he needed and not his own. This of course was so obvious that he felt thoroughly ashamed of himself.

So although he began his assignment with a great deal of trepidation, he was pleasantly surprised by the very first event that was blazed across the heavens for the angels in heaven and the men on the earth below. He wanted his very first headline in *The Heavenly Chronicle* to be so attention-grabbing that no-one, not even the evil powers who might also be alerted, could fail to sit up and take notice.

Chapter Two

With great anticipation, Raphael had been watching and waiting for this moment. He was expecting something amazing to happen. He had been told that an extraordinary prophecy was about to be fulfilled; that the King was about to be born. So for a few months now, he had been flying between luxurious palaces, hovering above some of them, trying to listen in on some of the ruling king's conversations, but so far he had learnt nothing.

"You will have to be very patient," Michael had said. "You will have to watch and listen; you will have to fly long distances, gathering important news that you can pass on to the heavenly realms. You will have to be selective: there will be so much going on that you won't be able to report on everything you see and hear. That will be impossible. I have assigned you this task because the Lord believes that you're the best angel for it. I know you won't let him down."

Raphael wanted to rise to the challenge. He really did. But so far, apart from the normal earthly strife and conflict, – domineering rulers, oppressed peoples, rigid rules, unspeakable cruelty meted out to disobedient subjects – all

Satan's work, for what could you expect from the Prince of the World – he had not seen any sign or heard any conversation that indicated where God's son was going to be born.

Even in Judea, where prophecy pointed, all was silent in the palaces. Perhaps he should broaden his horizons and look in other places.... the Chief Priest's residence? One of the Pharisees or Sadducees? Surely at least one of the teachers of the law? But all of them just seemed to be going about their normal business: endless council meetings, tithing at the temple and collecting tithes from the people, making sure that the Jews read the Torah, obeyed all the rules and commandments, presented the required sacrifices when they failed to do so. Although there were some murmurings about prophecy being fulfilled and the Messiah coming to rescue his people, there was certainly no mention of the imminent arrival of a baby boy who would become their King.

Because in Judea he was hitting dead ends wherever he turned, he decided to fly further afield – as far as the exotic Orient in the East. It was there that he uncovered his first surprise. It was while he was hovering above a great marble palace that the revelation occurred. And it was all to do with a star.

This particular palace boasted a domed observatory which towered above all the other palace structures. Round the full circumference of this domed building was a wide floor, rather like a deck, on which stood four imposing telescopes angled at the heavens. Had it not been for these telescopes, the palace, which was like so many others in the Orient, might have flashed by below his flying feet, unnoticed. But those telescopes attracted his attention, particularly as at the very moment that he flew above them, there were three men gazing intently up at the stars. There was an excited cry from one of them: "Balthazar, have you seen that star in the north-western quadrant?"

"Do you mean the brightest star in the heavens tonight, Ebenezer?"

"Yes, that very one. Truly, I have never in my whole career as an astrologer ever seen a star so bright."

"That is very strange."

"Not so strange. Remember the ancient prophecy: that on the night just such a gloriously bright star appeared in the heavens – a star like no other star that has ever been seen, or will ever be seen again – a great king will be born. A unique king. A king who will be worshipped by the whole world."

Raphael had stopped flapping his wings. He was trying to be as quiet as he could as he hovered above their heads, listening intently. At last, he was finding out something vitally important – news of such significance that it was essential to report it in *The Heavenly Chronicle*. If he hung around these kings, he was certain they would lead him where he wanted to go.

"A king of that calibre deserves our homage," mused Ebenezer. "Even if it takes years, I think we should go on a pilgrimage to find him. It will probably necessitate all our combined resources, for it will be a very long journey."

"If this great star leads us to the king who was prophesied centuries ago, he is a king like none other; he is the Saviour of the World."

"Oh Ebenezer, I am eager to find this king, for the birth of this child... this event... will change history." He paused, then said more practically, "Shall we begin to make our preparations in the morning?"

"That is a good plan. Within three days, we will embark on our journey to find the Saviour of the World."

Raphael waited until the three men had gone down below and the terrace with telescopes was empty. He then flew eagerly to the nearest telescope to see the star the three kings were talking about. When he looked through the powerful machine and discovered where the star was, he said aloud to himself: "You idiot, Raphael. Of course. The prophecy! The king will not be born in a palace, and it's Bethlehem where the Lord is sending him to be born. I've known of Micah's prophecy for centuries. Why didn't I connect it to this vital event – the first I will be reporting in *The Heavenly Chronicle*: 'But you, Bethlehem Ephrathah, though you are small among the clans of Judah, out of you will come for me one who will be ruler over Israel, whose origins are from old, from ancient times.'" (Micah 5 v 2)

There was that other prophecy from Isaiah that had always mystified Raphael: "The virgin will be with child and will give birth to a son, and will call him Immanuel" (Isaiah 7 v 14).

Who had ever heard of a virgin giving birth? But then his Lord and Master was a God of miracles: anything was possible for him; after all, he had created the whole universe, so of course permitting his own son to be born of a virgin was perfectly possible for him. It also made Jesus Christ distinct from other babies, who were all born tainted with the sin of the first man, Adam. There was no such blemish on God's holy and spotless son.

Raphael decided he had done enough reflecting. He didn't waste any more time. He flapped his wings furiously, flying as fast as he could through the night and the next day. Like any earthly reporter, he didn't want to arrive at this important event when all the action was over. It might take those wise men months to arrive at Bethlehem, but he, Raphael, was going to be right there when the birth of this important king, God's son himself, was to be born into the world. Clearly, this was the initial event that Michael wanted him to report. And he wanted to make sure he captured all the details as accurately and as colourfully as he could.

When he got there, he hovered around the place for a very long time, observing and learning. He admired the diligence of the shepherds in the fields watching over their flocks, he noted the learned scribes reading their Torahs and dispensing wisdom to the people and he saw the women faithfully preparing food for their families and doing other chores. But most of all, he waited with eager expectation for the event that would 'change history'.

Trying to keep his mind open, he scoured the town and the landscape for a potential birthplace for the baby. He found no family in Bethlehem who fitted remotely the profile of the holy family. It was only after he heard some men below him chatting about the census that he began to scrutinise the travellers who were flocking into the town. Of course – the whole population was returning to the place of their birth. So Joseph would be returning to Bethlehem to register for the census. Joseph with his wife Mary, who would be carrying a child.

Raphael was on the main road leading into Bethlehem when he noticed a tired man leading his heavily pregnant wife into the town. Her expression as she sat on the donkey was calm and serene, remarkable for a woman who was imminently to give birth. This couple was turned away from the first inn they came to. "Don't worry, Mary," said her husband as they were turned away from the second inn, "we will find a place."

"I know, Joseph. God will lead us to a safe place," she replied.

It was soon after this that an innkeeper told Joseph that he could use the stable, which was already occupied by sheep, cows and other donkeys. What a place for a heavily pregnant woman! And what a place for God's son to be born! But at least there was shelter and warmth there. A manger and hay was better than a cold cobbled street! And Raphael was delighted to see that the birth happened quickly. So quickly, in fact, that a multitude of his colleagues descended from heaven, winging towards a field occupied by shepherds who were looking after their sheep. Events happened so quickly that Raphael had no time to take notes for the first article he was going to write. The happenings unfolded so miraculously, though, that every detail was imprinted on his brain.

So later that night and with great enthusiasm, he began to pen his very first article. When the final draft was complete, he trumpeted it through the air to the heavenly printing press where the angels were waiting to announce and distribute the news throughout the heavenly realms.

Michael, reading the article the next day, gave him this compliment: "You have managed to record the events accurately. Well done. After one more article, you will have thirty years to hone your skills even further before the next crucial event will need to be captured. The angels and the devils alike will be captivated by your clarity." Raphael bowed his head in deference, acknowledging the senior angel's compliment; he vowed then and there never to disappoint his superior. Praise from this angel was more precious than all the gold and rubies in the throne room.

He read the article aloud to reassure himself that what Michael had said was true: it was a clear, well-expressed article, one of which he could be proud. It helped that the event itself was so newsworthy – more than newsworthy, in fact. The event was a matter of life or death for millions of people around the world, both in the past, in the present and in the future.

Prophecy finally fulfilled
The Saviour of the World was born in Bethlehem today

In the early morning of the first day of a brand new century, in the town of Bethlehem of Judea, a special baby, Jesus Christ, was born to Joseph and Mary.

The young couple had travelled all the way from Nazareth in Galilee so that Joseph, who belonged to the house and line of David, could register his family in his home town. Quirinius, the governor of Syria, had decreed that a census should be conducted of the entire Roman world.

But there was a particular reason for God's very own son, Jesus Christ, to be born in Bethlehem: the prophet, Micah, had foretold the most significant birth the world had ever known, or will ever witness, centuries before it happened: "But you, Bethlehem Ephrathah, though you are small among the clans of Judah, out of you will come for me one who will be ruler over Israel, whose origins are from old, from ancient times." (Micah 5 v 2)

The birth of Jesus was also heralded by a host of angels and announced by the appearance of a brilliant star which shone over the place where the baby lay. Surprisingly, it was a group of humble shepherds to whom Gabriel first proclaimed the good news of the Son of God's arrival into the world: "I bring you good news of great joy that will be for all the people. Today in the town of David a Saviour has been born to you; he is Christ the Lord. This will be a sign to you: You will find a baby wrapped in cloths and lying in a manger."(Luke 2 vs 10-12) It was these very shepherds who heard the glorious song of a whole host of angels as the heavens were filled with their voices praising God: "Glory to God in the highest, and on earth peace to men on whom his favour rests." (Luke 2 v 14)

The shepherds were so overjoyed that they hurried to the stable where the Christ-child lay. There, seeing that everything was just as the angels had said, they worshipped the child, rejoiced with his parents and eagerly went out to spread the proclaimed the good good news of the Son of God's arrival into the world. The magi from the East who had travelled from distant lands, followed the star which guided them all the way to Bethlehem. As soon as they reached this town, they went straight to the palace to enquire of Herod about the new king of the Jews. Herod instructed them to bring him news of this baby's birth, deceiving them by saying that he wished to pay him homage. With great joy, the magi took their gifts of gold, frankincense and myrrh which they presented to the child as they bowed down and worshipped him.

But before they could go back to Herod, an angel warned these magi in a dream that they should not go near his palace. Obediently, they went back to their own countries by another route. The God

of the universe was not going to allow anyone, let alone an insignificant king like Herod, to thwart his master plan of bringing a Saviour, Jesus Christ, into the world. The whole of mankind should be rejoicing at God's great gift, just as the angels across the breadth of heaven are doing. Our mighty Lord and Master graciously pours out his love on the whole of humankind as a great and glorious prophecy is fulfilled in the little town of Bethlehem.

Raphael
The Heavenly Chronicle

What Raphael didn't know was how speedily the words of his article had been trumpeted across the heavens. Nor did he know just how ecstatic the reaction in heaven was to the extraordinarily triumphant news that Jesus had been born in Bethlehem – and that the Son of God himself was on a mission to save mankind. Choirs of angels thronged around the throne room, lifting their voices in adoration and worship to the King of Kings and Lord of Lords. Their beautifully lyrical, tuneful harmonies remained uninterrupted for days and days and days. So eager were the heavenly beings to exalt and glorify their King that some of their other duties were put on hold for a while; their praise and worship was so infectious that Raphael learnt afterwards about all of them being completely caught up in it themselves. Hence, the resounding victory song flooded heaven for a very long time, only subsiding, in fact, when the heavenly host waited breathlessly for the next piece of news, which came soon after the birth itself; eight days, in fact. It happened in Jerusalem, when Joseph, like a good Jew, took his son to the priest in the holy city so that the baby could be circumcised in keeping with the law. Something so profound happened at this particular circumcision that Raphael couldn't wait to write his article, thereby proclaiming to the heavenly host just how significant Jesus' earthly life was going to be, especially as the importance of this new baby's birth had been noticed even by two earthly people, one of them a man, the other a woman.

The words bubbled out of him as he penned his article; the finished product was being trumpeted through the skies almost simultaneously to the time of the actual writing: the heavenly host celebrated in style with extra-special harmonies, the volume of their voices drowning out all other sounds in a hushed, attentively listening universe.

At Jesus' circumcision, Simeon recognises the light God's son brings into the world

Eight days after Jesus was born, as was required by law, Joseph took Mary, his wife, and Jesus, his newborn son, to the temple at Jerusalem for the rite of circumcision. As was required, Joseph gave the priest a pair of doves to sacrifice on the occasion.

The priest, an old man whose name was Simeon, appeared to be deeply affected by the baby he took into his arms, as he cried out in a loud voice: "Sovereign Lord, as you have promised, you now dismiss your servant in peace. For my eyes have seen your salvation, which you have prepared in the sight of all people, a light for revelation to the Gentiles and for glory to your people Israel." (Luke 2 vs 29-32) Mary and Joseph were clearly overwhelmed by what Simeon, this wise old priest, had said about their son, particularly as they discerned that his words were inspired by the Holy Spirit of God. Joseph looked intensely into Mary's eyes as they held each other's hands; Mary nodded in awe, but it was she, and not Joseph, who was next addressed by the priest. After blessing the child, he said to her: "This child is destined to cause the falling and rising of many in Israel, and to be a sign that will be spoken against, so that the thoughts of many hearts will be revealed. And a sword will pierce your own soul too." (Luke 2, vs 34-35)

Just then, an old prophetess, Anna, who lived in the temple, worshipping night and day, came up and confirmed what Simeon had said about the Christ child: "This Jesus will redeem Israel," she sang out. "Jesus, Redeemer of Jews and Gentiles alike. What a privilege to see this Redeemer-child with my own eyes. Thank you for bringing him to the temple on this special day." Joseph and Mary both smiled at the prophetess, but Mary held her hand to her heart. Clearly, she was wondering about Simeon's prophecy about the sword piercing her heart.

When everything had been done according to custom, Joseph and Mary left the temple with their newly-circumcised baby boy whom they had called Jesus, as the angel had said.

The ceremony of circumcision has taken Jesus one step closer to his mission of redeeming Israel, but we will have to wait for him to grow up before we can see God's faultless plan for the redemption of the world unfolding.

Raphael
The Heavenly Chronicle

He only learned much later about the impact both of his articles had had on the angels in the heavenly realms.

All he knew was that those two pieces he had written would have to stand alone; the circumcision article highlighting the significance of Christ's purpose and ministry on earth was to be the last article he would be writing for a very long time. While Raphael was anxious to write more articles, he respected Gabriel's request for relative silence during the next thirty years. This was very difficult for him; as a young angel, he had always been impulsive, and even now that he was more experienced, he still found it hard to control his enthusiasm, particularly if he thought he had performed a task well.

But above all, he was an obedient angel – he knew only too well the disastrous consequences of disobeying God. He had watched with horror as Lucifer and his followers had tried to act like God himself. Who were they to challenge their creator? So being thrown out of heaven and denied the very presence of God was a devastating punishment indeed, but a just and deserved one.

Raphael shuddered to think how those angels could possibly survive their cold, lonely fate. They had boasted to him on a number of occasions about their vast riches, their spectacular material wealth and their superior power. Of course, they were deluded, but their blatant selfishness and total disregard for the very maker of the heavens and the earth made Raphael disinclined to feel even an ounce of pity for these proud, defiant beings who had spat in the face of the very God who had given them life and breath. They deserved their horrendous fate: all the riches of the whole world were no compensation for their enforced separation from their creator – forever.

So despite wanting to make his mark on *The Heavenly Chronicle*, to shape his stories, spreading the good news and the amazing plan of God across the length and breadth of the heavenly realms, he knew he had to do his research, practise his writing skills patiently, restrain his urges to send off his articles before the appointed time and be self-controlled and alert as he grew to maturity. Waiting had never been his strong point, so the vista of the next thirty years presented an almost impossible challenge for him; entirely impossible had it not been for the strength of the Lord and the encouragement of his fellow angels.

Chapter Three

At the very moment that Raphael had been observing the baby Jesus in the midst of mankind and penning his articles about the Christ's birth and his circumcision, all the angels from one corner of the heavens to the other were lifting their joyful voices in melodious harmonies as they praised their Lord and God, the creator of the heavens and the earth, for the awesome works that his hands had made. From the north, resounding trumpets reverberated across the heavens as the choirs of angels sang: "Praise and honour and glory to the one who created light".

From the south, came the answering cry from the second massed choirs of angels: "Holy, holy, holy is the Lord God Almighty, the one who spoke, and it came to be. He commanded the light to appear, and it blazed forth in the heavens".

From the west, all the angels acknowledged that they had heard the praise and worship, and that they, too, wanted to pay tribute to their Lord and Master: "Hallelujah, hallelujah to the King of Kings and Lord of Lords. Mighty is the Lord God, creator of heaven and earth. Praise be to God for the beautiful brightness of his light." The resonating response was a chorus of multiple 'Hallelujas'; "Praise to our Lord God for his wonderful gift of light."

"Hallelujah. Praise, honour, glory and power to the Lord God Almighty for creating the glorious light. Hallelujah, hallelujah. Holy is our God."

As each new chant began, the volume of praise increased; at the crescendo of the angels' worship, their songs drowned out every sound in the heavens. But there were plenty of other things the angels wanted to praise God for. This time the eastern choirs began the worship, their songs of praise rippling and ringing from the east to the west, from the south to the north, so that all the angelic beings did not stop praising God.

"Hallelujah to the Lord God Almighty. Praise be to God for creating heavenly beings and giving us the beautiful name of angels."

"Hallelujah to our Lord and King. Praise him in the highest heavens."

"Praise him across the length and breadth of the heavens."

"Worship him all you heavenly beings. Worship him for creating the light, and for creating the angels. Honour and glory and praise be to him for evermore."

"Hallelujah. Hallelujah to the Lord Almighty, the King of the heavens."

"Praise God that he distinguished the light from the darkness."

"Worship the Lord in the beauty of his holiness. Hallelujah, hallelujah."

"Praise God that we, his heavenly beings, can see."

"Praise the Lord of the heavens for his glorious light."

32

As wave upon wave and chorus after chorus and song after song echoed from one end of heaven to the other, Raphael, far below on the earth, thought he heard a sound like the exquisite tuning of the spheres. He looked up to the heavens, which were at that moment bathed in a glorious light, and, pausing briefly from his task, he sang praises to his God. As he lifted his voice to the heavens, a great peace descended on his soul; for a moment he felt as if he was back in God's throne room with his fellow angels as, with one voice, they all paid tribute to their heavenly King. Feeling truly inspired and uplifted, he continued his waiting and watching with renewed vigour in his heart. Meanwhile, the angels didn't stop praising God for his magnificent creation.

"Praise God for creating the waters and the land."

"Hallelujah, hallelujah."

"Praise God for speaking the morning and the evening into being."

"Hallelujah, hallelujah. Praise Him. Worship Him."

"Praise our Lord for creating the land and the sea."

"Hallelujah, hallelujah."

"Praise God for creating the vegetation and the trees."

"Praise Him. Praise Him. Hallelujah, hallelujah."

"Praise God for making the sun, the moon and the stars."

"Praise Him. Praise Him. Hallelujah, hallelujah."

"Praise God for creating the creatures of the sea, the living creatures on the land and the birds of the air."

"Praise Him. Praise Him. Hallelujah, hallelujah."

"Praise God for creating man in his own image. Praise God for creating males and females."

"Hallelujah, hallelujah. Praise the Lord of all creation. Worship Him, all you creatures on the earth and all the heavenly hosts."

"Praise Him with instruments. Dance and sing to the Lord. Let us, together, celebrate the creation of the heavens and the earth."

Once again, Raphael, still at his post on the earth as he watched and waited, thought he heard the music of the heavenly spheres. Far away, in the heavens above his head, thousands of angels in God's celestial orchestra, in joyful assembly, made beautiful, harmonious sounds with their lutes, harps, lyres, strings and flutes. The blissfully peaceful, rhythmical music flooded the heavens as the angels praised God continuously with their instruments, their voices and their flowing movements.

Then, suddenly, at the blast of a trumpet, two sets of headlines, in cloud-like, wispy italic script, were formed in huge letters across the sky:

The Saviour of the world was born in Bethlehem today

and

At Jesus' circumcision, Simeon recognises the light God's son brings into the world

A new urgency emerged in the angels' songs and in their playing of their instruments. The louder, more majestic instruments were added to their celestial orchestra: the trumpets, the pipes, the horns, the tambourines and the cymbals. Now, their praise and worship was ringing across the heavens, resounding so loudly that even Raphael, who was so far away from the celebrations, distinctly heard the triumphant music and the words that were being repeated over and over again by thousands upon thousands of ecstatic angels: "Praise God that the Saviour of the world was born in Bethlehem today. Hallelujah, hallelujah. Praise God that the Son of God has brought light into the world. Hallelujah, hallelujah."

Raphael was filled with joy that he, as a humble instrument, was being used by God to spread such amazing news across the heavens. He was inspired to write and write, and send and send, praising God with his whole being. Truly, he felt completely satisfied; humbled to be of service to his creator God, the Lord of the heavens and the earth.

But sadly, this fulfilling, ecstatic feeling of pure joy was soon to be shattered as he continued to observe the earthly sons of men; Raphael would find himself wondering how on earth Jesus was going to be treated in this evil and sinful world.

Chapter Four

Michael had warned him he had a lot to learn. And he wasn't wrong. What he hadn't told him about was just how rife sin and corruption were on the earth. The angel, Lucifer, had fallen with all his followers as a result of the besetting sin of pride. Plenty of the earth's people seemed to have that, at least, in common with the arch-deceiver. But what was equally disturbing was how greedy most people on earth seemed to be: greedy for riches, greedy for power, greedy for sexual satisfaction. Men were clearly prepared to do anything to get what they wanted, including plundering, stealing, murdering and raping. And as he was flying around observing mankind, he was just looking at their outward actions; God only knew what was going on in their hearts.

It was all utterly depressing – almost more than he could bear. Despite the fact that he had undertaken to do his job – and his duty – as well as he possibly could… and that included all the research that needed to be done…he almost got to the point of asking Michael permission for a bailout.

One evening, when he had had a particularly bad day watching sin upon sin pile up in the most holy city of all,

Jerusalem, he speedily winged his way to Michael's quarters in the heavenly realms. Before he had even rounded the mountainous clouds and flittered down the lighted golden pathway to Michael's marble reception room, he was already calling frantically: "Michael, Michael… "

Patiently, but also long-sufferingly, Michael answered him: "Raphael, welcome to my abode – yet again. I am rather surprised to see you here… I thought you had an assignment on earth… "

"Michael, Michael," called Raphael again, even though he was now just a couple of metres from his superior, "this job is impossible… I… can only do it if that is what the Lord really wants of me."

Michael looked at him steadily, not displaying a hint of emotion as he responded: "In the Lord's strength, you can do any job."

"But Michael, with all due respect – I don't think you understand… it's a madhouse down there… there's so much blatant exploitation and suffering. I don't think I'll be able to observe all that for the next thirty years!"

Michael was disconcertingly silent.

"Man is so evil. You won't believe what they're getting up to: coveting, and stealing, and murdering, and raping. I could go on but I won't. It's too distressing…. "

He waited for a response, but still it did not come. With an infuriatingly passive expression on his gloriously shining face, Michael continued to regard him silently.

"You've been in the throne room, haven't you?" Raphael hadn't intended it to sound like an accusation. He paused. Still his senior remained impassive. "I mean, let's face it, it's pretty sheltered up here. You don't see the unspeakable atrocities taking place on earth... " He sighed, then tried, rather tentatively: "Wouldn't it be possible for me to be re-assigned... "

Now Michael did speak. Rather a long speech in fact. More like a lecture. But as a prelude to his oration, he firmly shook his head – three times, so even before he had uttered one word, Raphael already knew the answer to his urgent request: a resounding 'no'.

"I was one of the angels who announced the good news of the birth of the Messiah to the shepherds, remember. Although Gabriel was the chief messenger on that occasion, I was there, hovering above the earth, looking down on those humble shepherds, listening to Gabriel as he announced the glorious message that a Saviour had been born to them. Amazingly, not only to them, but also to all mankind. All mankind: past, present and those yet to be born. What magnificent news. What a privilege to announce it. I've also been around the world more times than you can possibly imagine. And I've seen what mankind is capable of. Why do you think men and women need a Saviour? Why do you think God's plan of redemption is so drastic: sending his own son into the world to fix humanity is an extraordinary act of love. Yes, there will be separation. Yes, there will be sacrifice. But it will all be worth it in the end. Because sin will be defeated. You just have to trust our Master. He can do it. He will do it... don't you think you could just play a very small part in the grand scheme of things? Think what a privilege that will be – to be obedient to the Master... "

"I'll do it," responded Raphael, by now feeling utterly ashamed of himself. "What was I thinking. I'm sorry. I'll get back to my task immediately, and I'll try, once again, to do it to the best of my ability. It'll be hard though – very hard."

"You seem to have forgotten something very important – again," scolded Michael. "Whose strength will you be using?"

"Not my own, that's for sure." Raphael allowed himself a little laugh.

"Of course not your own strength. It's God strength you – and mankind (if only they would open their eyes to see) – will need."

"I feel stronger already."

"Remember, God will defeat all sin, all evil. He has a master plan that I don't know about, but I trust my master to bring it to fulfilment at the proper time."

"Thank you for the encouragement and the guidance. I can see just how much I need to trust the Lord of the universe. I'll get back to work."

"Just to lift your spirits, I'll send you out into the world with a resounding melody in your ears."

At that very moment, a host of angels who had descended from above lifted their trumpets. They played an exquisite melody which consisted of one triumphant note heaped upon another until, at last, Raphael was out of earshot as he sped through space down to earth to observe the sons of men.

Chapter Five

He winged straight to the place where Jesus had been born:
Bethlehem itself, the place of celebration where the angels had
so triumphantly announced the birth of the Messiah. For
sentiment's sake, he headed for that special stable where the
baby had been born to Mary, with Joseph, the shepherds and
of course the animals – mostly donkeys – looking on. Except
for the animals, he found it empty. He had been expecting that.
What he hadn't been expecting was the blanks he kept
receiving when he tried to locate the abode where the child,
his mother Mary and his father Joseph, were living. He flew
over house   after house; he even landed on a few of the flat
roofs where people chose to sleep on hot nights and listened in
to their conversations. But he heard nothing about the baby
Jesus, and nothing at all about Mary and Joseph.

Becoming frustrated with searching the ordinary abodes
of men, he decided to travel south to the king's palace in
Jerusalem. Perhaps the king had recognised the baby's
importance and invited the family to stay in one of his many
capacious apartments. Even as the thought crossed his mind,
Raphael chided himself for being naive. This was the Roman

Empire he was considering: the brutal conquerors of many, many nations, who, although they permitted their subjects to practise their own religions, still controlled their public life. The powerful emperor and his appointed rulers brooked no opposition, clamping down ruthlessly at the slightest hint of rebellion. With great shock, Raphael had noticed all the crucified bodies lining the main roads. These Romans appeared to stop at nothing to enforce subjugation on the people they conquered.

So, with a revised expectation of what he would find in the palace, but still hoping for some news, Raphael sped his way to the Judean seat of power. The massive size of the palace was visible from a long way away: the building seemed to stretch on and on – Raphael did find himself wondering what an earthly king of a very small kingdom needed with so much space. As he got closer, he could see that the human king had attempted to make his palace as splendid as possible. Of course this earthly palace paled into insignificance next to the glorious richness and resplendence of the Lord's heavenly abode, but it was still pretty impressive.

Because it was constructed on an elevated platform and rested on a series of retaining walls, it towered over all the other buildings in Jerusalem and was, with the exception of the temple, the most impressive structure for miles around. Firstly, there were the three immense towers which surrounded this forbiddingly fortified palace. These tall towers were constructed of massive white marble blocks which glinted in the sunlight. The palace itself was walled, but spaced at equal distances all around the wall were other towers. The roof of the palace was made up of very long beams, and was adorned with splendid ornaments and statuettes.

When he hovered over the palace, he noticed that there were two main buildings; on closer inspection, he saw that no expense had been spared on the interior: there were banquet halls, bath complexes, as well as enormous bedchambers containing beds for hundreds of guests apiece. At the centre of the palace there were beautiful gardens, the grounds including groves, canals adjacent to dove-cotes consisting of tame pigeons, ponds decorated with bronze fountains, porticoes, several groves of trees and long walkways lined with distasteful statuettes where water gushed out of orifices.

As Raphael had noticed that there was much activity in one of the banquet halls, it was behind a pillar there that he decided to hover, hoping that he would pick up significant news from the conversations of some of the guests. He was disappointed, however. The men reclining on the couches were so busy stretching out their right arms again and again and again to take hold of a variety of delectable treats that kept being loaded onto the tables: lamb, beef, chicken, duck, geese, hares, pigeons, turtledoves, partridges and young goats. But all this, Raphael learned, was only the first course. Afterwards pigs were brought to the table; pigs stuffed with thrushes, duck, warblers, pea puree, oysters and scallops. Later the guests feasted on roasted boar and oxen. Copious amounts of wine in large bowls kept being delivered. Distasteful as Raphael found all this gorging and drinking, gluttony wasn't the only sin the sons of men were blatantly indulging in. Lust, another of the seven deadly sins, was being paraded for all to see: while naked girls danced provocatively amongst the guests and troupes of acrobats tumbled among swords, breathed fire from their mouths and acted out obscene parodies, men were leering, lurching and grabbing, some of them successfully, at the alluring naked bodies swaying luridly before them.

Raphael felt that he had watched and listened long enough. So disgusted was he by all the promiscuity and decadence he had witnessed that he could not stay here on the mere chance that anyone there would mention that baby boy who had been born in Bethlehem. He had caught just one snatch of conversation about the recent slaughter of all boys under two who had been born in Bethlehem. How depraved were these sons of men! And yet it was part of Raphael's assignment to watch them carefully, to gather information and to record their actions thirty years from now. He knew he could not possibly desert again; he had steeled himself, this time, to do his duty whatever depraved actions he had to witness. But it was going to be very hard for him, especially as he knew that the atmosphere in the heavenly kingdom was peaceful, loving, beautiful and productive. What a contrast to this earthly life! Why would anyone want such a life of discord, violence, depravity and horror? What had happened to men's consciences? Raphael gave a small shudder as he flew around in a circle rather aimlessly, wondering where he should go next.

It was then that he remembered the words from Isaiah: "A shoot will come up from the stump of Jesse; from his roots a Branch will bear fruit." (Isaiah 11 v 1) He smiled as he thought about the clever word play on the Hebrew word, 'netzer'. Of course... Nazareth.... that's where he must go. That's where he would find Jesus and his earthly family and where he should be concentrating his time. He felt elated as he winged through the scudding clouds, the river Jordan winding across the land far below him. Michael had hinted to him about the significance of that famous river but he hadn't been specific: time would unfold the importance of the river on his own mission. Meanwhile, he intended to gather as much background information as he could relating to the clearly evil world where his Master, the God of the whole universe, had sent his son.

But as he racked his brains for a biblical verse which would guide him to the right place, he had a revelation. In mid-flight, he stopped flapping his wings so hard, put on the breaks and did a neat turn, heading in the opposite direction. Egypt! As clear as daylight now. He even had a flashback to the warning that had been given to Joseph by one of his colleagues. The man had been told to flee to Egypt to escape the slaughtering of the baby sons. But it was the prophet Hosea's voice that was ringing in his ears as he flew swiftly to that ancient land where Joseph had worked his way up the ranks from slave to second-in-command: "When Israel was a child, I loved him, and out of Egypt I called my son." (Hosea 11 v 1)

It was when he was flying over the Sinai desert that he heard a furious flapping of wings above his head. He looked up to see Michael, a golden light radiating from his pure white robe.

"Stop!" commanded the high-ranking angel.

Greatly surprised by this unexpected visit, Raphael lowered his wings, merely flapping them gently to sustain his airborne position. Michael never visited the earth unless he had an important message to relay or something significant had happened which required an urgent response. So it was with apprehension that Raphael prepared himself to hear his senior's message.

"What are you doing here?" demanded Michael.

Innocently, Raphael responded, "What I'm supposed to do: I'm collecting information."

"You do realise you're off-course," responded Michael, a slight hint of sarcasm in his tone.

"No I'm not." Raphael's tone was defensive.

At that, Michael gave a deep sigh which sounded like a strong wind. "Raphael, Raphael. You have much to learn. You are very young – enthusiastic, yes." He gave a fond smile. "But you will have to learn patience... and restraint. You can't just fly off here, there and everywhere. You need to focus on the holy land itself."

"But... "

"You also have to learn obedience!" thundered Michael.

What could Raphael say to that? Guiltily, he looked down.

"Let me remind you of your research assignment," he said, softening his tone. "It is to gather as much information as possible about the land where God's son will be carrying out his earthly mission."

Nervously, Raphael said: "May I ask a question?"

"Of course," replied Michael benignly.

"As Jesus' family is now in Egypt, why doesn't my assignment include a visit to that ancient land, the land of Moses and the Israelites?"

"Because apart from fulfilling prophecy, it is not as relevant or important as the land of Israel. So you are to turn back right now and continue your research according to the brief that was specifically created for you."

"In the absence of the holy family?"

"Yes. I have it on good authority that they will not be in Egypt for very long." He paused, allowing his words to sink in."Oh, and Raphael…" he said it almost as an afterthought. "When you get to Israel, you will have as much freedom as you like. You will be guided to the places you are to visit, but you may also use your own initiative. It is only in thirty years' time that it will be important for you to stay strictly on course again."

"But how will I know?"

"You will know. The events will speak for themselves. Now turn around, go back to Israel and do your job properly. You need to educate yourself – thoroughly – about the lives of men."

Michael's wings, which had, like his, been steadily pulsing, now accelerated as he prepared to ascend to the heavens. There was no time to ask him any more questions. In an instant, he had propelled himself speedily through the air and was now only a speck on the distant horizon. Raphael was left hovering in the air, still awed by the impressiveness of God's most significant messenger.

He had the strongest urge to follow Michael up into the heavens. The 'education' he had been instructed to subject himself to was one he could do without: it would be so much easier to sing praises to the glorious king of the ages, to watch him conversing with the saints, pouring blessing after blessing upon his people and spreading his majesty, peace and contentment wherever he went. But this earthly research was so completely different. Oh, it was a beautiful world all right: the creator had made extensive green forests, plunging ravines, majestic mountains, surging seas, pearls of islands, broad winding rivers, scudding clouds, twinkling stars, brilliantly bright suns. Dazzling though the heavenly realms were, the earthly beauty that Raphael was witnessing at close range took his breath away. If his assignment had been to focus merely on the natural splendours of the world, he would have been in his element. But unfortunately, his assignment was to observe the sons of men; to get as much background information about not only the men who were the earthly rulers, but also about all the people who inhabited the earth, in particular, those who lived in Israel. Of course, he also had to focus on the place where God's son had been born, where he was to spend his earthly life and the temple in Jerusalem.

It was true that Mary, Joseph and Jesus had had to flee to Egypt to escape the wrath and jealousy of King Herod. But while this was most significant for fulfilling prophecy, it was not particularly relevant for his assignment. He had been tasked with learning as much as possible about the land and people where Jesus was to live during his earthly ministry. Distasteful though this was, he decided to investigate from the top down – from the palaces and residences of the rich, powerful and influential. He planned to do this as systematically as he could, by first examining the lives of the king and other governors, then looking into the high priest and the religious leaders and the way they lived; and only then going on to scrutinise the daily lives of ordinary men and women.

Of course he had already witnessed all the decadence and greed associated with the king's palace. To his shame, that is what had motivated his attempt at abandoning his duty... to break free from his unpleasant earthly assignment. He had so badly wanted to be reassigned to even the most humble of tasks in the Lord's heavenly kingdom, so desperate had he been to escape from all that blatant sin and complete disregard for God's law by the vast majority of humankind, from the greatest of men to the least. But Michael had reminded him of his obligation to the living Lord of the universe.

So here he was, flying swiftly through the air to the very seat of depravity: Herod's palace itself. As he already knew the layout of this magnificent mansion, complete with its massive walls, towers and security features, he knew exactly where to go to find out more about Herod's heart: in his council chamber where all the major decisions of the state were made. But he didn't find Herod in his council chamber. Not one adviser could be seen there. The chamber was completely empty. In fact, despite the relatively early hour – God's sun was still shining brightly in the heavens – Herod and all his advisers were in the main banquet hall indulging themselves in what was obviously their favourite occupation: feasting, or more accurately, gorging. Raphael found himself turning away at the site of all these grown men stuffing their mouths with delicacies while semi-naked women weaved their way around their couches, dancing seductively and posing suggestively.

Raphael had to steel himself for this ordeal. He told himself that it would be cowardly to flee again. If he wanted to gain any understanding of the motives of this corrupt king, he would have to hover above him, out of sight behind one of the many huge statuettes and pillars that bordered the banquet table and its surrounding couches. Just a precaution. He had been told that men couldn't see angels in the earthly realm, a fact that mystified him, especially as angels frequently conversed with the saints in heaven; so he was covering his bases – just in case. There were, after all, precedents: Abraham who had met three 'men' at Mamre; Jacob who had seen angels ascending and descending the ladder to heaven; the angel who had led Moses; Daniel who had witnessed the angel shutting the mouth of the lions in the den so that he remained unharmed; Balaam who could not see the angel standing in his way until the Lord opened his eyes; and the servant of Elisha whose eyes were opened so that he could see the hills full of horses and chariots of fire all around Elisha – the army of the Lord. What a pleasure it was to think about these holy men of God. And what a contrast they were to King Herod, his advisers and his guests at this banquet. But Raphael knew that he would have to listen intently and sift through all the bawdy comments to get to the heart of this king's intentions which, with all the earthly power he wielded and the huge labour force at his fingertips, could be converted into instant actions. And he also knew that it was important for him to obey the Lord's instructions to the letter; the name of the Almighty King of the universe must be glorified at all costs.

Raphael found King Herod downing a goblet full of wine. When he had finished, he held it up in the air, expecting it to be filled immediately – which it was – by a young girl clad in a seductive, low-cut, flowing silken red robe. With one hand he stroked her shapely form as she bent low over him to fill his goblet. But he soon tired of flirting with the girl. He was more intent on boasting about his achievements.

"So you see," he announced loudly to his assembled guests, "I will go down in history as the king who built Jerusalem."

He laughed uproariously, then gazed around the room, expecting an appropriately awed response from the whole company. When it didn't seem to be forthcoming, he bragged all the more loudly: "Even the Jews have me to thank for their magnificent temple; as king of the Jews, I insist on allegiance from this people, so building a temple for them doesn't hurt! I have noticed how the Sadducees are deferring to me... And who else could have given them solid gold on their walls and brilliant limestone which shines so brilliantly... only Herod the Great. And as a symbol of the might of Rome... suggesting the presence of all the legions and the supremacy of Rome, who placed the golden eagle at the very entrance to that temple? I – I alone." Here he thumped his chest, then turned his head to speak to the nearest guest: "Who gave the Jews their beautiful temple and their mighty golden eagle which they can worship?"

The response was instant: "Herod the Great," echoed his compliant guest, eyeing the heavily-weaponed guards who were stationed at every entrance and exit.

"Who gave the Jews their temple and their mighty eagle?" Herod now challenged all his guests as he cast his beady eye around the room.

"Herod – Herod the Great," came the thunderous response.

Smiling broadly, Herod continued to bask in his glory: "And who built the Antonia fortress in Jerusalem?"

"Herod the Great," chorused the guests.

"And the palace – and the theatre – and the amphitheatre?"

"Herod the Great," thundered the guests.

"And who built the temple at Caesarea Philippi to honour great Caesar?"

"Herod the Great."

He waved his hand around. "I will continue to build Jerusalem, and the whole of Judea. I will continue to be the greatest king Judea has ever seen." He paused. "And I have also given you culture." Here, having swigged back another goblet of wine, he burped loudly. "The culture of the Greeks goes hand in... hand –" he slurred – "with the might of the Romans. More wine –" he demanded, holding out his goblet – "you, feed it to me... " He grabbed the girl's arm and pulled her towards him, so that her breasts were squashed against his copious chest.

Raphael decided he had seen enough. So he rose into the air, deftly ducking through a doorway, fluttered up a stairway, through an open window and out into the sun-drenched skyline. Resolving to leave the avaricious, proud king to his own folly, he decided to seek out the high priest's residence. Surely he, at least, would demonstrate the purity of his office to the world.

Chapter Six

The first thing Raphael noticed about the High Priest's quarters was that they were in the upper city of Jerusalem where the wealthy lived. His home was surrounded by the residences of the rich, famous and influential. The second thing he noticed was the spaciousness of the place and the lavishness of the decorations: its mosaic floors, ritual baths, ordinary bathtubs, reception halls, frescoes on the walls and ceilings and exquisitely crafted pottery were all evidence that this man, himself, was in favour with the Romans or they would not have permitted him to live in the lap of luxury.

He found the high priest taking a walk in the massive courtyard around which all the rooms were clustered. He was in earnest conversation with another priest who, judging from his attire, was also a Sadducee.

"We must ensure that every pure Jew who steps across the threshold of the temple pays the required temple tax," he said. "Some of our priests are failing in their duty by not enforcing the payment of this tax on everyone."

"As you are aware," replied the priest, "some exceptional cases have been brought before your very Council. It is my submission that the Sanhedrin should consider the financial circumstances of our men in certain cases... our populace is over-burdened with taxes... "

"The law requires that everyone pays his tax," replied the High Priest severely. "It is an insult to God to deny him his due. We cannot allow laxity in this area. I believe there are also some priests who are permitting certain purification rituals to slide. This is totally unacceptable. Every male must have his ritual bath before he enters the temple. I absolutely insist that this law is adhered to. We cannot allow the 'unclean' to come into the very presence of God. Moses would not have allowed it. Aaron would not have allowed it. These are God's standards we are dealing with. Then there is the matter of the sacredness of the Sabbath. Certain men have been known to carry their mats to the very verge of the temple. You know they are not allowed to work on the holy Sabbath. We will have to tighten up – on our own priests and on the populace. People are becoming slack, and God will be displeased."

"May I be permitted to raise the subject of the golden eagle at the very gates of the temple? The people are becoming restless."

"It is not for us to question the wisdom of King Herod. Remember that he built the temple for us – so we will have to make some allowances. Now tell me, what is the order of the day? We must both ensure that we do our duty by our Almighty God."

"There are five ceremonies to perform relating to ritual purity. The women are coming out of their menses and will be bringing the necessary sacrificial animals."

"Aaah, doves and pigeons. That will take up most of the morning. What else?"

"We also have some ritual baths to supervise: two men buried their brothers and will need ritual purification. You will then need to convene the court... the full body of the Sanhedrin needs to hear the cases of three men who are accused of working on the Sabbath day. I also have to report that two of our members have been contaminated by dining with the Gentiles."

"Will our people never learn! It is vital that we, as a Jewish nation, remain pure. We cannot tolerate men in our midst who insist on defiling themselves by associating with the Gentiles. They must be cast out! Our national identity as a Jewish nation is at stake!"

"One man even lay with his wife at the forbidden time of the month."

"That is unforgivable!" shouted the High Priest.

"He insists that her flow had not begun when he began the act... "

"They all say that! He will need to be the first case tried by the full body of the Sanhedrin. That man is a stain on our nation and must be cast out. A full programme in service of the Lord! But how important it is that we are stringent about this. God forbid that anyone 'unclean' should pass through the portals of our sacred temple due to our negligence. Let us go and prepare to fulfil our duties."

The two men disappeared through an archway. Raphael took a deep breath. What burdens the High Priest was placing on the ordinary men and women of the community. He decided that he must go and see for himself how those over-taxed people lived, and how they were bearing up under the heavy burdens that were being constantly imposed on them. He found a sorry state of affairs: people living in dire poverty; many families and their friends were living sixteen people to one room; the children appeared to be sadly under-nourished. Women scoured the ground for grass and roots to bring home so that their children could at least have something to eat. One family was wailing because the husband and father had been recently carted off to a debtor's prison. But some opportunists took the line of least resistance, buying the right from the Romans to become tax collectors in order to cheat their very own people. And this was the world into which Jesus, God's own son, had been born!

To cheer himself up, Raphael decided to visit the shepherds. They were, after all, hard-working, honest men who earned their bread with their days of labour in the field. They, at least, could support themselves with food and clothing from the animals they so meticulously cared for: fleeces from the flock and meat and milk from the animals. And it was to the shepherds in the fields at night that Gabriel had brought the great message of the birth of their Saviour.

Raphael knew exactly where he needed to go. No kings, high priests or tax collectors for him now. He was going to observe the sons of men who lived more modest lives, particularly as the Christ had been born into the family of a humble carpenter.

As he had been particularly impressed with the joy of the shepherds as they worshipped the King in that Bethlehem stable, he decided to visit these very men in their rustic abode. Swiftly, therefore, he winged his way to the hillside in

Bethlehem where Gabriel had announced the news of the Saviour's birth. Although he flashed past two young boys out in the open as they guarded their flocks, one of them who was playing a sweet melody on a reed pipe, he flew straight to the sheltered spot where a cluster of mud huts hugged the hillside.

When he noticed an old man reclining on a mat in the centre of the hut, he hovered, as he felt the need to hear what he was saying to the man who was bending over him.

"No more jackals will get at the flock?" asked the old man, concern furrowing his brow.

"We'll all fight to keep them away," the man replied. "That's why both boys are watching tonight."

"But Jethro's so new to this... I hope he doesn't fall asleep."

"His brother will see to that," laughed the younger man gruffly. "Right now, he's keeping him awake with his music."

"I thought I heard the sound of the pipe," sighed the old man.

"And Jethro's also calling to the sheep. I heard him crying out their names... Pure White, Striped, Black-Brown, Gray-Eared..."

"That'll keep him busy," chuckled the old man. "You taught him well."

"That I did! And even though he's just helping his brother, it was a good idea of yours to kit him out with his own equipment."

"Every shepherd out in the field, no matter how young, needs his stout bag, rod, bucket and sling."

"I hope those boys don't have to chase away any hyenas tonight!" remarked their father.

"Our great God will protect them from the wild animals if they come," replied the old man. "Remember how he saved David from the lions and other wild beasts on the prowl."

"He is like a shepherd to all of us," replied the man. "The greatest shepherd in the world."

"That is why I don't fear death."

"Oh Father... don't talk of death tonight."

"Old Seth is very ill... and very weak... " laughed the old man. "You know that – and you know that I will not be much longer on this earth."

"It's terrible to think of these things!" protested the old man's son. "Let's talk of something... remember that day, Father, that we left the flock in the care of the boys and took our sacrifices to the temple... "

"That was a very long journey," mused the old man, rallying his strength as he remembered.

"All the way to Jerusalem! But our fellow shepherds looked after us on our travels."

"Yes – gave us beds of straw, fed us, treated us like kings."

"But the best was when we got to the temple."

"Aah – that psalm of David... I'll never forget it."

Raphael could hear the intense emotion in Seth's words – even though by now his voice was soft and faltering.

"Sing it with me now, Father."

"I... you... sing," he rasped as he struggled to breathe.

It was then that Raphael witnessed something remarkable. With every word of the familiar psalm that his son intoned, the old man seemed to be striving to get closer to heaven. As each beautiful word spilled out from his son's lips, he appeared to be lifting himself off the earth and straining, stretching, reaching towards some rich prize just beyond his reach.

Raphael himself wasn't immune to the comforting tenor voice of this man as he sang, boldly and confidently, those wonderful words David had composed such a long time ago:

"The Lord is my shepherd,
I shall not be in want.
He makes me lie down in green pastures,
he leads me beside still waters,
he restores my soul.
He guides me in paths of righteousness
for his name's sake.
Even though I walk through the valley
of the shadow of death,
I will fear no evil.
for you are with me;
your rod and your staff,
they comfort me.
You prepare a table before me in the
presence of my enemies.
You anoint my head with oil;
my cup overflows.
Surely goodness and love will follow me
all the days of my life,
and I will dwell in the house of the Lord for ever."
(Psalm 23)

So passionate had Seth's son been about singing the beloved words he had memorised that day in the temple that he hadn't noticed the change in his father's body. One moment

Seth had been thrusting out his arms and reaching skywards; the next he had collapsed in a heap, seemingly hanging on to life by a thin thread.

The song finished. When the son did finally turn to the father, he cried out in alarm, "Father, Father." Frantically, he shook the almost lifeless body of his father.

"Son, I... " At that moment, all the life seemed to go out of Seth's body. His head dropped to his chest, his hands hung lifeless and his limbs stiffened.

"Father. Father... " The shepherd was desperate. He shook the now lifeless body, but it only slumped again. "Noooooo – don't leave me."

There was a deafening silence.

"Boys... boys... " he shouted. "Come quickly. Come now."

Incapable of deserting the old man's body, he cradled it in his arms, rocking back and forth, back and forth, back and forth, shouting and screaming so loudly that the boys did, finally, rush into the hut. Immediately, the youngest burst out, "Why's grandpa smiling?"

It was at this point that Raphael experienced an unexpected surprise. But not before he observed an angel of comfort hovering near this man and his children.

Just then, a bright light filled the heavens and Michael stood above Raphael.

"You have done enough for now," the angel announced. "God has recalled you to the heavenly kingdom for the foreseeable future – that is, until you are needed on earth again. You have been reassigned your former duty of welcoming the saints into the heavenly kingdom. Especially the most recent addition to the kingdom," he added, gesturing to Seth's lifeless body.

"That's wonderful!" Raphael couldn't help smiling broadly. "When do I start?"

"Immediately."

"And how long will it be before I am needed on earth again?"

"Thirty years," Michael confidently replied.

"Thank you, gracious Lord," he said, praying to heaven. "I will do my best in all things to honour your name."

"But remember, when the time comes, you will be sent back to this earthly kingdom for three years. Then your job of serious reporting for *The Heavenly Chronicle* will continue."

"I will be ready for it!" replied Raphael enthusiastically. "Because the next thirty years will be a wonderful privilege; they will give me a respite from the troubled earthly realm. I will be better able to handle the problems when the time comes."

"Hallelujah!" remarked Michael.

Happily, he journeyed to the heavenly realms to take up his former position at the entrance to his Lord and Master's supreme council chamber. What a privilege it was going to be to welcome the saints once again into the awesome and resplendent presence of God himself. And now that he knew at first-hand what they had to endure to achieve their own personal crown of glory, he would have far more respect for these earthly saints. He was going to appreciate every single moment of what he considered as his respite period before going into the earthly battleground.

The very first job assigned to him in the heavenly realms was to welcome Seth, the new shepherd saint who had so recently given up his earthly body. How wonderful it was to see Seth's glowing face as he entered the tunnel of light. And to note the smoothness of his skin, the youthfulness of his appearance and the energetic spring in his step. For Raphael, the first time of observing the transformation of a saint on earth to a saint in heaven was more amazing than he could possibly have imagined. Seth's upright, healthy body was a sight to behold, but even more impressive was the radiant gleam that exuded from his whole being. What Raphael was witnessing was perfect joy, perfect fulfilment, perfect contentment. And when Gabriel himself met Seth at the entrance to the heavenly kingdom, so overwhelmed was he that he dropped to the ground and lay prostrate before the glorious angel. But immediately, Gabriel said authoritatively, "Worship the King only. I am merely his messenger. Rise, my son." Obediently, Seth rose. "Welcome to the Lord's home. It is good to have you with us. Raphael will introduce you to our heavenly choirs."

Still radiating joy, Seth replied, "It is a great honour and privilege to be here. God is very gracious."

"The full extent of his grace is being worked out right now on the earth you have just left."

A light appeared to dawn in the shepherd's eyes: "The king has been born!" he cried.

"In Bethlehem. In a stable," confirmed Gabriel.

"And you were the angel who announced the news," replied Seth excitedly.

"Glory to God in the highest, and on earth peace to men on whom his favour rests," (Luke 2 v 14) intoned Gabriel. As each word was repeated, Raphael witnessed Seth's face glowing even more brightly.

"That birth will change the world," he said softly.

"I wish more sons of men thought so," commented Raphael.

"We shepherds saw what happened," continued Seth. "We felt the presence of the Almighty. We worshipped the King in that stable."

"And now that you are in the king's domain, Raphael will show you around," replied Gabriel.

With great enthusiasm and also a fair amount of awe, Seth, who was obviously surprised and delighted that he could sail through the air on his transformed and strengthened pair of legs, followed Raphael as he led him to the chief heavenly choir master. Raphael didn't waste any time in announcing the arrival of this new saint: "I have a new recruit for you," he remarked, "Seth, the shepherd. Strong bass voice."

"Once had a voice!" laughed Seth. "My voice is old and cracked now, like a broken, torn drum."

"Sing what you like singing best," said the choir master.

"What, now?" asked Seth in obvious alarm.

"Yes. Lift up your voice."

The chief choir master's command had a hypnotic quality about it. Immediately Seth began to sing in a totally restored voice: a deep melodious bass.

"God made the land, he created the sea,

He formed the sun and the moon and the stars in the sky. He made animals tame and wild... the sheep in the fields and the jackals in the forest...

He spoke. The sea was filled with wonderful creatures – like the great leviathan which swam in the oceans...

But the most amazing thing of all he made was – me."

The last line of this song was delivered with such gusto that Raphael couldn't help smiling at this new saint's enthusiasm. Especially when the heavenly choir master, with a loud trumpet blast, gathered the choirs from one end of the heavens to the other to join in this exultant creation song. Seth looked around in amazement at the mass of gloriously shining angels who were clustered around him, their wings outspread and their voices raised in perfect harmony. The sopranos and mezzo-sopranos, the tenors and the base singers were all grouped together for maximum harmony; the angelic choirs elevated Seth's simple shepherd's song into an operatic tour de force fit for a king – for the king, the king of the whole universe, who, with the breath of his mouth, had formed everything.

Raphael felt as if he was watching a grand spectacle: so appreciative was he that instead of participating, he flew round and round in circles, trying to take in the blending of voices and the skill of each section of the choir.

The most wonderful thing of all was to watch Seth's face. He seemed so surprised at the glorious way in which his song had been transformed that he was looking all around him, as if he was a child experiencing the harmonious voices of a superb choir for the very first time. The expression in his eyes was one of innocent joy, and so intent was he on listening to the beautiful melodies that were filling the heavens, that he had stopped singing as he allowed himself to be immersed in the waves of music.

The massed choirs' improvised rendition of Seth's song was followed immediately with a magnificent 'Gloria' that metaphorically raised the roof of the heavens.

"Glory to God in the highest,

Hallelujah, hallelujah;

Glory and honour and praise to the King of Kings and Lord of Lords;

Hallelujah, hallelujah.

Majesty and power and dominion belong to our great God and King,

Creator, ruler and sustainer of all things,

Hallelujah, hallelujah."

Raphael experienced this uplifting praise not only washing over him, but also pouring into the deepest reaches of his soul. He wasn't, however, in such ecstasy that he failed to notice how much Seth was being affected by these glorious harmonies. His face had been radiant before, but now it was lit up like the sun, reflecting the brightness of the angels in his vicinity.

The sublime praise continued to lift the spirits of all the angels and saints present, particularly of the new members of the heavenly realms to whom this exceptional calibre of worship was a novelty. Not only was the quality of the music – both instrumental and vocal – sublime, but also the wholehearted adulation of the instrumentals and massed choirs pointed to a sincere, focused and concentrated commitment to praising and worshipping and honouring the King of Kings and Lord of Lords.

Raphael observed that Seth was becoming more and more emotional with each rich bar of the superb music. He had clearly experienced nothing remotely like this ever before. Music he had heard while in his earthly body – even at festival occasions at the temple – was a pale reflection of the magnificent music he was hearing now. By the time the angel in charge of feasts had circled the ranks, loudly announcing the news of a banquet, Seth was almost on the point of swooning with ecstasy. Raphael flew close to him, softly encouraging: "Seth, you have been invited to the banquet."

In a dream-like state, Seth whizzed through the air, obediently travelling to exactly where he was led, a place about halfway down a scrumptiously-laden table. But appetising though the feast looked, it was not the food – its quantity or delicacy – that created a striking impression on the new saint; it was the company.

"I am placing you amongst your fellow shepherds," said Raphael.

The angel didn't have to introduce Seth to the illustrious company. The man's startled exclamation as he instantly cried out the names of those men seated nearest to him at the table spoke for itself: "Abraham! Moses! David!"

"Welcome to the promised land," said Moses.

"The land God our Father promised us would be flowing with milk and honey," continued Abraham.

"A shepherd's paradise, fit for a king," added David.

"I… am just a humble shepherd… " stammered Seth. "But you… mighty kings, great leaders of God's people… "

"And shepherds like you," replied David. He paused. Then, turning to Seth and giving him a glowingly reassuring smile, he said, "It will be so good to talk about shepherding with one who has so recently left the flock. Were you still having such trouble with predators during the night when you tended your sheep?"

"I wasn't able to tend the flocks any more – old age, bad health – but my son and grandsons did the job after me."

"You must have been a good role model," David remarked.

"I passed on all I knew to them. I did what I could, but for the last few years, it was really hard."

"Do you remember those goats?" Moses reminisced.

"What problems they gave us with those long ears! We were forever patching them up."

"Those thorns and briars!" added Abraham.

"A shepherd's life isn't easy. At the beginning, I found that my flock wasn't even obeying me," said Moses.

"And oh, how much time and patience it took to build a relationship with the flock," said David.

"Now that was really important, and something I kept telling my boys," said Seth, warming to the conversation. "I showed them the best caves to hide in so the jackals and hyenas didn't get to them. And I taught them to talk to the animals so they didn't get into a panic. And of course I stressed how important it was to count the animals and to check their health often."

"What would we have done without our sheep!" said David.

"Their wonderful coats kept us warm in winter," agreed Abraham. "They certainly kept us clothed and fed. And gave us many other blessings."

"But didn't any of you get restless during your long nights under the stars?" asked Seth.

"We had our reed pipes for that," replied David. "We knew how to keep ourselves from falling asleep."

"You must have made up some of your psalms while you were looking after your sheep," said Seth.

"Like the Lord is my shepherd, Thou shall not want?" asked David.

"Yes, yes. Everyone must know that psalm," replied Seth.

"But not everyone really listens to the words," replied David.

"Let's sing it right now," said Moses enthusiastically.

"Round this banquet table? Right now?" asked Seth.

"Why not? Let the heavens resound with the shepherds' psalm," replied David. "So the heavens can be filled with God's glory."

Seth complied, and the feasting and singing went on for a very long time.

When the exalted praise had died down a little and there was a pause in the proceedings, Seth, once again, looked admiringly at David: "But you didn't only tend sheep on the mountains and in the fields," he said. He paused. David patiently waited for him to continue. "You shepherded the whole flock of Israel!"

David smiled modestly. "Not quite the whole flock."

"But it was foretold – long ago," added Seth. "I heard it in the temple when I went with my sacrifice."

"I felt the weight of my responsibility when I heard Ezekiel's prophecy for the first time," admitted David.

"Say it for me – please," Seth responded eagerly.

"It was all God's doing, not mine," said David. "I was just a humble shepherd boy, the youngest in my family, tending the flocks while all my older brothers were fighting against a powerful enemy."

"The Philistines," beamed Seth. "I loved the way you used your sling and a stone to defeat that proud giant of a Philistine."

"It wasn't I who defeated that Philistine," replied David. "It was God. He has always been my good shepherd… protecting, sustaining and guiding me."

"But please say those words from Ezekiel," pleaded Seth.

"Those words have lived with me," replied David, briefly closing his eyes as he reminisced: "I will place over them one shepherd, my servant David, and he will tend them; he will tend them and be their shepherd. I the Lord will be their God, and my servant David will be prince among them." (Ezekiel 34 vs 23-24)

"And that one about the King?" encouraged Seth.

"My servant David will be king over them, and they will all have one shepherd." (Ezekiel 37 v 24) Of course, they didn't always want me as their shepherd – and I wasn't always the perfect shepherd either."

"We all had flaws in the earthly kingdom," said Abraham. "But we knew how dependable our true shepherd was, just as our descendants did."

"And now that we know those glorious words from Isaiah, it's clear how we were strengthened in our weakest moments and comforted in our darkest hours," said Moses.

"Please say the words," said Seth. "I love to hear the words of God."

Moses immediately complied: "The passage from Isaiah speaks to my heart, so I will bless this company with those special words from the Scriptures:

Here is your God!

See, the Sovereign Lord comes with power,

and his arm rules for him…

He tends his flock like a shepherd;

He gathers the lambs in his arms and carries them close to his heart;

he gently leads those that have young." (Isaiah 40 vs 10-11)

"How can we ever thank our great God enough for all he has graciously done for us," said David.

"And continues to do," added Moses. "He graciously keeps pouring out his love for us, which we don't deserve, but… "

"He has promised to pasture his flock himself. He has promised to 'rescue them', to 'gather them from the countries', to 'tend them in a good pasture'," mused Abraham. "But his most wonderful promise is this:

'I myself will search for my sheep and look after them.As a shepherd looks after his scattered flock when he is with them, so will I look after my sheep. I will rescue them from all the places where they were scattered on a day of clouds and darkness.." (Ezekiel 34 vs 11-12)

"The Lord's power and might, his compassion and graciousness, is far, far beyond our understanding," said Moses. "But our great God is worthy of praise and honour and glory." At that very moment, Moses spontaneously dropped to his knees. All those close to him followed suit. So right there, in the middle of the banquet, the saints showed their appreciation for all their heavenly Father had done for them: "Father God, you are worthy of the highest praise and honour and worship and glory," began Moses.

"You are King of Kings and Lord of Lords," said David.

"You are the great shepherd of your flock," said Abraham. "You know each one by name, and you tenderly care for them, especially for the frail and the weak."

"You search for the lost and you find them," said David. "And you guard them, and guide them, and keep them, all the days of their lives."

"What a great privilege it is to be numbered as one of your sheep," said Abraham.

"Thank you, great Father, for bringing me into your glorious kingdom," said Seth.

As Raphael cast his eyes down the banquet table at all the feasting, praying, singing, worshipping saints, he thought about how good it was to be back home. Heaven was a place where all the angels and all the saints experienced indescribable joy. Apart from this celebratory banquet, right now there were at least a dozen ecstatic reunions taking place as the new saints were reunited with friends and families again. And when they met fellow worshippers they had been forced to say goodbye to because of sickness or death, there were exultant shouts.

But when one of his colleagues ushered these saints into the very throne room of God, the experience was so sublime and so awesome that without exception, all these saints dropped onto their knees and prostrated themselves on the glistening multicoloured floor. Many of them stayed there for a long time, not daring to lift their heads, allowing the glorious worship to swirl around them, infusing their whole beings with adoration and praise for their King of Kings and Lord of Lords. And Raphael could fully understand their reactions. No matter how many times he had entered that magnificent throne room filled with the very presence of God himself, he never failed to wonder at the majesty and might and power and love of his gracious and merciful God. What a privilege it was going to be for him to escort Seth, this humble shepherd, into the throne room for the first time.

For some saints like Moses and Isaiah, the first place they were taken to by the angels who had been assigned to their orientation was the throne room. But others, like Seth, the shepherd, received a more gradual introduction to the splendours of his King. The blinding light and radiating glory that shone forth from God himself would have overwhelmed him had he gone straight there. Raphael had been carefully noting Seth's reactions to the heavenly choirs, the great banquet, and his introduction to three great men of God, to see if he was even remotely ready to be ushered into the very presence of God. Was anyone ever ready?

Suddenly, warm gusts of air, like tumbling waves, propelled Raphael forward. Michael, who had stopped abruptly just above him, was waiting for his attention.

"It is time," the angel said.

"For the throne room?"

"Yes. The shepherd saint is ready to meet the Lord," Michael replied. "Will you please escort him there immediately."

Raphael responded by smiling broadly. What a privilege it was once again to be going into the very presence of God. He didn't waste any time carrying out this special mission.

"Seth," he said, touching the man on his shoulder with one of his wings, "you must leave the banqueting table now. I am taking you somewhere very special."

"Couldn't be much more special than this!" laughed Seth good-naturedly as he looked at the laden table and the throngs of saints who were feasting and conversing, filling themselves not only with food fit for kings, but also with conversation fit for angels.

"Follow me," said Raphael.

"Where are we going?" he asked as he sped easily after his guide.

"To the holy of holies… "

"Do you mean…?"

"It is time to meet your creator, Seth. The Lord and King of the whole universe."

"But… I… "

Raphael got behind the hesitant Seth and propelled him gently forward until they stood at the very threshold of the throne room itself. Clearly responding to the blinding light and glorious radiance that shone resplendent from the throne room, Seth shut his eyes. But the brilliant light wasn't the only reason for his tightly shut eyes. He was bending his head forward, at the same time swaying sideways on his feet as he listened intently to the rhythms and harmonies of the seraphs' hymns of adoration. Impulsively, Raphael joined in with the uplifting praise: "Holy, holy, holy is the Lord Almighty; the whole earth is full of his glory." (Isaiah 6 v 3)

So powerful were the voices of the seraphs that the doorposts and the threshold shook mightily. The elders in the throne room responded to the seraphs' praise by bowing before their Lord and singing, "You are worthy, our Lord and God, to receive glory and honour and power, for you created all things, and by your will they were created and have their being." (Revelation 4 v 11)

Seth was so stunned by this magnificent praise that he didn't open his eyes for a very long time. When, finally, he did, he cried out in awe and dropped to his knees. Unlike some of the other new saints who were so overwhelmed that they prostrated themselves and failed to rise until they were actually lifted off the ground, this humble shepherd, although remaining on his knees, seemingly could not get enough of the glorious vision in front of him. His eyes were huge, his mouth had dropped open, and his arms were raised in worship. Well might he marvel at the sublimely heavenly image before him: the sparkling sea in front of the throne, as clear as crystal; the six-winged seraphs flying around the throne; the throne itself that had the appearance of a sapphire; the rainbow-like radiance surrounding the throne; and the almost indescribable Lord God himself, from his waist up looking like glowing metal, and from his waist down appearing like red-hot, brightly-burning fire.

Then Raphael heard a deep sound emanating from Seth's newly-restored voice, and was moved to hear his spontaneous praise – the simple shepherd's song that the full choirs of angels had so recently transformed to a magnificent anthem:

"God created the land,

He created the sea.

He formed the sun and the moon – and the stars in the sky.

He made animals on land – tame and wild…

the sheep in the fields and the jackals in the forest…

He spoke – and the sea was filled with wonderful creatures like the great leviaithan which swam in the oceans…

But the most amazing thing of all he made was – me."

Seth remained on his knees for a very long time, still gazing in awe and wonder at the majesty and glory and radiance of the Lord seated in the distance on his sapphire throne. Occasionally, he shielded his eyes from the light of the blinding crystal sea which reflected the glory of God on his throne. But the more he knelt there, the more he appeared to get used to the brilliance in front of him. His smile was growing broader as the hymns of the seraphs circled around him.

Then, quite suddenly, he rose from his knees, lifted his arms and in a deep, rich bass, he echoed the seraph's songs: "Glory to God in the highest, Hallelujah, hallelujah." He repeated this chorus over and over again, his tone becoming more and more enthusiastic with each word that he uttered. The atmosphere in and around the throne room was electric: every seraph's or angel's song was so dynamic that Seth began to dance. As his rejuvenated legs stamped and swirled, he spontaneously sang about his earthly sheep, mentioning them one by one as he thanked God for protecting them:

"Oh great shepherd, thank you for saving Pure White from the wolf,

Thank you for guarding Striped from the lion,

Thank you for pulling Black Brown from the pit,

Thank you for shielding Gray-Eared from the leopard."

At the end of his praise song and his wild dance, he dropped to his knees once again, bowed his head and prayed: "You are truly an awesome God, the great shepherd of the sheep."

The seraphs' and angels' songs, although continuous, dropped slightly in volume as this humble but beautiful prayer wafted like incense to the very throne of God.

For the briefest of moments, there was a hushed silence, a flurry of wings and a whoosh of air as one of the seraphs flew to a point just above Seth's bowed head. Gently, he tapped the shepherd's shoulder with his wing. Seth looked up, startled.

"Our Lord and Master wants you to see something," the seraph announced. "Raphael, you are to take this shepherd to the celestial pasturelands."

"Oh, he will like that," Raphael responded.

"You are to follow your guide," commanded the seraph, looking authoritatively at Seth.

Unquestioningly, Seth strode speedily through the air in the exact path of his angel guide. Together, they travelled past circles upon circles of glitteringly golden mansions, orchards upon orchards of abundantly laden fruit trees and gardens upon gardens of fragrantly flowering blossom trees and exotically coloured shrubs, until at last they reached their destination. Seth, in sheer amazement, was replicating Raphael's expansive revolutions around a vast green, carefully tended grassland. But it wasn't only the excellent quality of the pasture that was astounding Seth; he was clearly completely overwhelmed and delighted by the harmony amongst the animals. For a conscientious shepherd who had spent all his working life on earth protecting his sheep and goats from prowling skilful predators like jackals, hyenas, wolves and occasionally even lion and leopard, he was overjoyed at the friendship and even love displayed between the wolf and the lamb who were peacefully grazing side by side, the leopard lying languidly with the young goat, and the lion and the young lamb strolling across the grasslands together, occasionally gambolling amongst the straw.

So revolutionary were these scenes before him that Seth, once again, broke into spontaneous praise: "O Lord God, ruler of the heavens and the earth, you alone can bring together the wolf and the lamb, the leopard and the goat, and the lion and the lamb. Hallelujah, hallelujah. Praise and glory and honour to the King of Kings and the Lord of Lords. The angelic response in the form of reverberating praises across the heavens was deeply satisfying not only for Seth, the humble shepherd and new saint, but also for Raphael – who was well aware that the reprieve he had been granted from viewing the sons of men and reporting on the Son of God's actions as he walked among men was only temporary – thirty-years temporary to be exact. And what was thirty years when viewed from a celestial perspective? Gone in less time than a flash of light.

So Raphael made sure that he milked every moment of his thirty-year sojourn in the heavenly realms: he sang, he danced, he praised; he showed Seth around the glorious landscape that was the heavenly kingdom, including the twelve trees that represented the twelve tribes of Israel which bordered the river of life itself. Every time he was given the privilege of introducing a new saint into the wonder of the heavenly kingdom, he was deeply humbled and awed by the experience; he knew he would never tire of this type of work, but he also knew that there were less pleasant tasks that every angel was expected to do with joy on occasion. So when that quick flash of thirty-years had come and gone, he was completely ready to do his duty on earth again, although he did experience a pang leaving that shepherd saint Seth and his colleagues behind in the glorious kingdom of his Lord and Master, the great and glorious God of the universe.

But there was one great consolation: to observe the Son of God himself at close quarters as he walked amongst the sons of men.

He was deeply conscious of the privileged task that had been placed in his hands, and was eager to carry it out to the best of his ability.

Chapter Seven

Even so, his 'respite' had past far too quickly, chiefly because he had enjoyed himself so much. When the time finally came for him to go back to earth, the moment for serious reporting of events had begun. But this time, his job was more specific: unlike the last time when he had been 'gathering information' in a general way about the rulers and the people of the earth, specifically of Judea and the surrounding areas, this time he was told to follow Jesus around, select some events that he considered to be significant, and relay them via *The Heavenly Chronicle* to the inhabitants of the heavenly realms. He was excited about the challenge, especially as it involved observing and learning from the Son of God himself.

As he got closer to that shimmering orb – its large patches of blue marking the position of the oceans – its flecks of green covering indicating where the forests were – he reflected, once again, on the sheer beauty of God's creation. The land masses were now more distinctive so, guided by their shape and form, he headed for familiar territory: the area around Judea. On his last visit to earth, he had loved watching the river Jordan winding through the landscape, so he flew freely over the river, appreciating the way the water was in harmony with the vegetation and the associated agricultural activities.

It was only when he neared the region of the Judean desert, where the vegetation around the river became extremely sparse, that he noticed a long line of people snaking towards a wild, long-haired man who was adorned with animal skins; this man was systematically submerging people in the river. He remembered the words of Michael when he had asked how he was going to select significant events and most importantly, how he would know that the time was right. Michael had confidently asserted: "Oh, you will know." He looked more closely at the people in the line. It was clear from their clothing and indeed, from their very bearing, that there were some men – and, to Raphael's surprise, women – of rank. But the vast majority of those who were awaiting their turn to be baptised (because clearly, that was what was happening here) were the tradesmen, the poor, the everyday men and women of the land.

Most of the people were talking quietly amongst themselves as they waited patiently for their turn in the river. There was, however, one group of wailing women who cried out loudly, "John, John, we have sinned. Baptise us. Cleanse us. We are unclean." They kept up this cacophony until a tall, bearded man with a dignified bearing approached John across the desert sand. The women instantly became quiet: their eyes followed this stranger; they were clearly fascinated by the man and calmed by his presence. John pointed to him and cried out in a loud voice: "Look, the Lamb of God, who takes away the sin of the world!" (John 1 v 29)

The people were astonished. All eyes were now turned to the stranger who had been identified in such an unusual and mind-blowing way by John. Raphael was now hovering above their heads, very close to the main actors in this drama. Clearly, something extremely significant was about to happen. Something eminently reportable. Something all creatures in the heavenly realms would want to know about. And it was he, Raphael, who was at this very place, at this very time. He felt extraordinarily privileged. He held his breath as he waited expectantly.

What did happen was so remarkable that it took him some time to process the significance of the event. At the time, his pen had gone into automatic writing mode – he had written copious notes in his own brand of shorthand. He realised how important it was to relay information as accurately as he could so that God, the Lord of the universe, and his very own son, Jesus Christ, could be glorified by the heavenly hosts. So, aware of his responsibility to all those heavenly beings who were waiting to hear news of God's son, he boldly wrote down a headline for the front page of *The Heavenly Chronicle*:

The Holy Son of God baptised in the Jordan

For a moment, he considered whether to include the prophet John's name in the headline, but then he decided against it. Headlines were all about focus; and the focus of this article must be on Jesus at the beginning of his ministry on earth. So he went with his original headline and began, in a careful, considered way, to write the first of his articles in this, his second mission to the earth.

The Holy Son of God baptised in the Jordan

Jesus Christ, who had travelled on foot all the way from Galilee to the Judean desert, was baptised today in the river Jordan by the prophet, John.

John, as was his custom, was immersing people in the river Jordan, announcing that this baptism in water was a sign that they must repent of their sins. Both high- and low-ranking men from all over Judea stood all day in the hot sun waiting to be baptised by this popular prophet. There were even some women in that long line which snaked its way all the way to the horizon. But the women stood apart from the men, for in Judea, it is not considered appropriately moral behaviour to associate too freely with women in public or open spaces.

Jesus, the Son of God himself, walked slowly across the desert sand towards John. John paused, stretched up and pointed towards the Christ, saying in a loud voice: "Look, the Lamb of God, who takes away the sin of the world." (John 1 v 29)

Some of the people standing nearby were bewildered as they frowned in puzzlement, but without exception, everyone turned and stared at this dignified, calm presence: the man who was approaching John who stood on the very verge of the river Jordan. Jesus leant towards John and said: "I have come to be baptised in the river Jordan."

Hastily, John replied: "Master, it is not right that I, a sinful man, should be baptising you."

Jesus immediately replied: "It is proper for us to do this to fulfil all righteousness." (Matthew 3 v 15)

So John submerged Jesus in the water. It was when his head was lifting out of the river Jordan that a dramatic series of events occurred: heaven miraculously tore open, leaving a gaping void in the sky. A beautiful white dove descended on Jesus, alighting on his head. Simultaneously, a loud voice from heaven announced: "This is my Son, whom I love; with him I am well pleased." (Matthew 3 v 17) Some men I spoke to when it was all over said they had heard an extremely loud peal of thunder, but I distinctly heard those words from above.

John, the prophet, also gave his testimony to the waiting crowd. In his own words: "I have seen and I testify that this is the Son of God." (John 1 v 34)

What a powerful way to begin a ministry on the earth. Jesus' identity as the Son of God has been confirmed by the great prophet, John, and reaffirmed by God himself speaking from heaven itself. This event bodes well for Jesus' mission in the world.

Raphael
The Heavenly Chronicle

After witnessing this ground-breaking announcement about who Jesus was, Raphael expected that at least some of the people standing nearby would show due reverence. But nobody seemed to be taking any notice of this crucial declaration. Mostly, they were just pushing forward in their line so that they, too, could be baptised by the prophet, John.

Raphael couldn't believe how dull of heart they were and how lacking in understanding. And he was also taken aback by the Son of God's next move: instead of going immediately to work amongst the people, he walked off, alone, into the desert. Obviously, the road ahead was not going to be easy. What would Jesus do, alone, in the desert? The answer, of course, was that he would fast, pray and get ready – physically, mentally and spiritually – for his earthly ministry. Raphael witnessed his forty-day preparation with great awe, but what really impressed him was Jesus' calm refusal to fall into temptation when, exhausted, hungry and vulnerable – as any other man would have been – he stood his ground against the devil by decisively beating him at his own game.

Chapter Eight

On a number of occasions during the next forty days and nights, Raphael was completely awed by what was happening below him in the Judean desert. Jesus had nothing to keep him warm on the freezing desert night except for the coats of the wild animals who would nestle up to him, providing a bed for him. This reminded Raphael so much of the scene of the nativity. Just as the wild animals in the desert protected him, so those donkeys and cows which had surrounded the holy family, sheltered them from the cold air in the Bethlehem stable. And the Lord's self-discipline was so inspiring. He rose early and drew enough water from a nearby well for his daily needs. As soon as he had finished his first drink of the morning, he went onto his knees, praying to his Father. Sometimes, he spent the whole day on his knees, breaking off only occasionally to sustain himself with the water that he had drawn from the well that morning.

But what amazed Raphael most of all was that in all the time that Jesus was in the desert – for forty long, hot days and forty long, freezing nights – he did not once put any food in his mouth. Raphael had seen how men could gorge themselves on the choicest meat, fruit and other delicacies... just one look at King Herod's table had convinced him of how much men seemed to crave food. And at the other extreme, he had watched the prophet, John, catching locusts to eat and foraging for wild honey. But not the Christ. He drank his water, daily, because he must have known that without its sustaining qualities, as a man, he would not survive in the desert. But as he clearly knew that he could do without food to survive, he steadfastly fasted, as always, keeping himself pure and faultless, but at the same time and in a paradoxical way – since his body, lacking food, was weak – he was deliberately strengthening himself, through constant prayer and fasting, for his earthly ministry.

By the end of those forty days, Raphael could see that his Lord and Master was fainting with hunger, but he also knew that he could do nothing to help Jesus physically unless he called out to the angels to fetch him food. And this he would not do. Jesus' resolution was truly remarkable. His flesh was weak, but his spirit was stronger than it had ever been, even when he was in the heavenly realms with his Father.

To his horror, Raphael observed the chief fallen angel, Lucifer himself, advancing towards Jesus at the very moment that he had knelt down for his morning prayers on this, the fortieth day of his desert ordeal. Obviously the arch-evil angel, who audaciously called himself the King of this world, was bent on tempting what he considered to be the weak and vulnerable body of Jesus. Raphael journeyed closer and listened intently to every word that Lucifer spoke, and every single word of Jesus' reply. Not for one moment did he believe that Jesus would succumb to temptation, despite his extreme hunger and the dire state of his physical condition, but he wanted to learn about how the Lord triumphed over temptation. He knew that the news of this encounter that was taking place in front of his very eyes would soon be recorded in *The Heavenly Chronicle* and emblazoned across the heavens. He also knew how important it was for him to record this meeting between the perfect Christ and the arch-evil deceiver as accurately as he could.

While he was listening, he found himself shocked to the core that Satan freely used the holy scriptures to justify himself, in Raphael's opinion, "feebly" attempting to prop up his earthly – but very temporary – power, with the very words of God himself.

With a beating heart, Raphael observed the drama unfolding below him, a drama which, some time later, he recorded delightedly in his second celebratory article for *The Heavenly Chronicle:*

The Son of God triumphs over temptation

Jesus Christ, the Son of God, has decisively demonstrated that he does defeat the devil. After fasting for forty days and forty nights in the inhospitable Jordanian desert, Jesus was very hungry. Because not one morsel of food had passed his lips during this whole period. Instead of searching for physical food, he had spent his time on his knees searching for spiritual food as he prayed to his Father.

That duplicitous fallen angel, Satan, decided to take advantage of Jesus' apparent vulnerability. What a coup it would be for him if he could persuade the Son of God himself to fall into temptation! So that deceitful master of lies had the audacity to quote the holy scriptures in his attempt to gain the upper hand.

Stealthily, he approached Jesus, sneering as he watched him kneeling humbly before his Father. Sensing his presence, Jesus opened his eyes and stood up, resolutely ready to face his enemy. Smiling slyly, the arch-tempter held out a large stone to Jesus. Pretending to be concerned about Jesus' physical condition, Satan said to him: "If you are the Son of God, tell these stones to become bread." (Matthew 4 v 3) Jesus looked straight into his tempter's eyes, replying: "It is written: Man does not live on bread alone, but on every word that comes from the mouth of God." (Matthew 4 v 4)

Satan spat on the ground in disgust, but he wasn't finished with Jesus. "Come with me," he said, "I want to show you something amazing." Calmly, Jesus went after Satan, climbing a steep mountain until he had reached the very top. Satan spread his arms widely, and strangely, in that instant, a variety of lands and kingdoms and palaces flashed by below them. Proudly, Satan said, "All these splendid lands, kingdoms and palaces that you see before you belong to me – they were given to me by your very own father! I am the supreme ruler over all of them. But I am such a generous angel. I am prepared to give all of it away. I will sacrifice all the authority I have over all these grand kingdoms. All you have to do is to bow down and worship me, and my treasures – every single one of them – will be yours."

Without hesitating for a moment, Jesus once again looked directly at Satan, saying firmly: "It is written: Worship the Lord your God, and serve him only." (Matthew 4 v 10) The devil couldn't help himself: he stamped both his feet in frustration, but he soon recovered his apparent equanimity as he craftily came up with yet another temptation. Judging by the sick smile playing across his lips, he obviously thought he would get Jesus this time.

"Come with me to Jerusalem. I will take you to the holy of holies, the temple. There, I know you will be at home."

Jesus said nothing, but he did follow his tempter, knowing only too well that Satan was not leading him to Jerusalem for his benefit. He would have discerned that he must prepare himself for a third temptation – all the way to Jerusalem, he was softly murmuring a prayer to his Father.

When they arrived at the temple, the devil wasted no time in saying: "Come with me and I will show you how magnificent your father's temple is. Come with me to the very top of this wonderful building."

Up, up and up they climbed, until they had reached the very top. "Now," Satan said, a cunningly triumphant expression on his twisted face, "if you are the Son of God, throw yourself down. For it is written, 'He will command his angels concerning you, and they will lift you up in their hands, so that you will not strike your foot against a stone.'" (Matthew 4 v 6)

Calmly and commandingly, Jesus replied: "It is also written; 'Do not put the Lord your God to the test.' (Matthew 4 v 7) Realising that he had been decisively defeated this time round, Satan skulked away. At last it was time for angels from heaven to flood to the Master's side, strengthening him and comforting him but most of all, praising him.

For in the Judean desert, on top of a high mountain and in the holy of holies, God's temple in Jerusalem, the Son of God had triumphed over temptation. He had conquered the arch-deceiver, forcing his enemy to retreat until an opportune time arose.

He was only forty days into his earthly mission, and yet Jesus was already demonstrating that he was worthy of his Father's trust as he began his difficult mission on earth physically, yet not spiritually, separated from his Father.

Raphael
The Heavenly Chronicle

Chapter Nine

A host of angels had been waiting at the ready to wing to earth the minute they were called by the Son of God. But Jesus had stoically refused to use his power to enlist their help. As a man, he had faced dire temptations with patience and steadfastness. He had not fallen, so when the angels received this report, the heavens resounded with adulation and praise for the Christ's victory over the devil. From the moment the chief trumpeters blared the news across the celestial sky and the wispy headlines were blazed across the heavens from one end to the other, all the choirs tuned up for an extended period of rejoicing.

Jesus' conquest of the fallen angel was particularly awe-inspiring because it showed that he was the one person who, when tempted, could defeat sin decisively. Ever since Adam and Eve had been thrown out of the garden of Eden for disobeying God, men and women had been seriously sinning through the ages: extreme violence and profanity of every kind – the savagery of rape, the brutality of murder and genocide, the barbarity of pornography and the horror of idol-worship all seemed to flourish across the face of the earth. Greed, covetousness, pride and the wish to dominate other human beings, subjecting them to all manner of abuse, were rife across the face of the earth. And yet Jesus had overcome his enticing temptations so purposefully that Satan had been forced to flee from him as he sulkily admitted defeat.

If only other men could follow Jesus' example and stand up steadfastly to the tempter when he enticed them, sometimes subtly, to disobey the law. Perhaps if they spent more time studying the word and less time obsessively compiling their own stringent laws which were impossible to keep, they would not be trapped so often into sin by the beguiling temptations of the arch-evil one. And perhaps if men stopped following their own evil desires and depended more often on the Lord of the universe, they would not fall so often into disobedience and depravity.

Jesus' triumph over temptation was truly earth-shattering and life-changing for those who would care to notice. It was a particularly potent message for all the remaining angels across the heavenly realms to remain pure and holy, and not to be deceived by any heavenly being who tried to rise above his station, as that wicked angel Satan had done. Pride and the yearning for glory had resulted in the spectacular fall of Lucifer and all the angels who supported him; an object lesson for any being who felt inclined to disobey the Lord and creator of the whole universe. That the Son of God, in his earthly body with all its limitations, had chosen to stand firm in the face of compelling temptations – that arch-enemy, the devil, had even had the temerity to quote the Holy Scripture for his devious purposes – was a worthy cause for celebration. So it was no wonder that the triumphant sounds that circled the heavens had such volume and such exquisite harmonies – the deep, rich voices of the bass singers, the fine-tuned voices of the tenors, the soothing sounds of the alto tenors and the uplifting vocals of the sopranos. One and all, they were joyfully singing about the amazing event that had just occurred on the earth below: the Son of God had truly triumphed over temptation, defeating Satan in the process and causing widespread rejoicing which reached every corner of the heavens. A defining moment on earth. An exulting series of celebrations in heaven. For these celebrations went on for a very long time.

Meanwhile, Raphael was continuing to gather more information about Jesus' ministry on earth. He noticed that as well as spending time in prayer to his father, attending the temple and reading the word privately, he was also walking around among ordinary men, mingling with them and attracting quite a crowd of followers. But the men who clustered around him weren't the type of people you would have expected Jesus to call to him: they were 'ordinary' working men – fishermen, labourers, men who worked with their hands.

Raphael watched, fascinated, as the Christ, the very Son of God himself, went about calling his first disciples – not princes, learned men or teachers of the law, but 'ordinary', un-schooled men, the kind of men who helped their fathers in the family business. Of course, thousands of men, women and children were already clustering around Jesus. His teaching was so different from that of the Pharisees and Sadducees; instead of telling the people to obey law after law after law, many of these laws not even written down in the word of God – laws which they, the Pharisees, had invented – this supreme

92

teacher, Jesus, told the people stories which related to their everyday lives; he taught them using plenty of colourful examples, often referring to a text from the word to support what he was saying to them. This 'man', as the people said, was a man who taught 'with authority'. What he told them was radical, and very different from the things they heard from the traditional teachers of the day. That was why he was already attracting such large crowds who loved to follow him and to sit at his feet, listening attentively to every word that he uttered.

Early one morning, as he was hovering above the Lake of Gennesaret, Raphael saw Jesus walking by the side of the lake. People were crowding around him, trying to make sure they heard every word he said about the word of God. Jesus, Raphael saw, passed two empty boats, but a little further along the shore, he discovered the occupants of the boats washing their nets.

"Simon," he said as he got into one of the boats, "please can you take me into the lake so that I can teach the people from the water. Then everyone will be able to hear what I say."

"Of course, Master," replied Simon, obligingly launching the boat into the water, but making sure that it was close to shore so that the people on the bank would be able to hear what this teacher was saying. Jesus taught them for a very long time, using words that they could understand, including everyday examples so that they could apply what he said to their own lives.

When Jesus judged that the people had had enough – they were tired and could not take in too much more teaching, he said to Simon: "Put out into deep water and let down the nets for a catch." (Luke 5 v 4)

Raphael expected this burly fisherman to obey the Master immediately. But to his surprise, the fisherman immediately objected. Clearly he didn't yet understand to whom he was listening. "Master," Simon said, "we worked hard all night – but we didn't catch a single fish. But I will listen to you. I will let down the nets just because you told me to."

So Simon took the boat further out into the lake, away from the crowds, and manoeuvred the heavy net into the sea. Almost immediately, the fish began jumping. A dark line of fish was streaming towards the place where Simon had put down his net. Soon, there were so many fish in the burgeoning net that Simon had to call his partners in the other boat to help him lift it from the sea. The men from the other boat also let down their nets, and soon, the same thing happened to them. Their nets were so full of fish and their boats so heavy with the weight of hundreds upon hundreds of fish that the boats began to fill with water. Watching patiently for the events to unfold below him, Raphael felt like giving a shout of joy when he noticed the reaction of all those fishermen to what had just happened. And he was touched by Simon's reaction. Simon, in awe and amazement, actually fell to his knees and appealed to Jesus: "Go away from me, Lord; I am a sinful man!" But Jesus, showing great compassion and understanding, said: "Don't be afraid; from now on you will catch men." (Luke 5 v 10)

Simon's companions were also amazed and couldn't stop marvelling at the extraordinary event they had just witnessed. Clearly, this Jesus was no ordinary teacher. Not only did he teach 'with authority', but he was also capable of doing extraordinary things. They must have thought that he was, at the very least, a great prophet who had come to enlighten them all about the word of God. Amongst Simon's companions were James and John, the sons of Zebedee. These men, following Simon's example, pulled their boats up to shore. They left their father and followed Jesus. Obviously, they thought, they could learn a great deal from this extraordinary prophet. They had much to learn about Jesus – chiefly that he was the Son of God himself. Raphael did wonder how long it would take them to realise that life-changing truth. Andrew, Simon's brother, also followed Jesus, as did Philip and Nathanael, who followed soon afterwards.

Nathanael's initial attraction to Jesus was prompted by what was actually no more than an ordinary exchange of pleasantries between two men. Except that this was a conversation with a difference: Jesus hinted that he knew a lot more about Nathanael than he could possibly realise: "Here is a true Israelite, in whom there is nothing false," (John 1 v 47) Jesus said about Nathanael.

"How do you know me?" was Nathanael's amazed reply.

"I saw you while you were still under the fig tree before Philip called you." (John 1 v 48)

Raphael exulted when he heard Nathanael's reverent reply. This was a man who understood the truth about Jesus – so early on in his ministry – that boded well for the Christ's mission on earth.

Nathanael's exact words thrilled Raphael's heart: "Rabbi, you are the Son of God; you are the King of Israel." (John 1 v 49) Raphael also felt extremely blessed to hear the Messiah's inspiring reply: "You believe because I told you I saw you under the fig tree. You shall see greater things than that… I tell you the truth, you shall see heaven open, and the angels of God ascending and descending on the Son of Man." (John 1 vs 50-51)

In fact, at that very moment in heaven, the angels were still celebrating their Lord and Master's victory over temptation. So continuous was their praise that it was only when the next amazing event concerning Christ's life on earth was reported to them that the angelic choirs paused to listen and to comprehend in wonderment and fascination.

But while all this celebrating was going on in the heavenly realms, Raphael was continuing to hover above the earth, winging this way and that – between Bethlehem, Nazareth, Jerusalem and the Jordan river – searching for the next newsworthy event in the life of Jesus of Nazareth. Of course, there were plenty of events on which he could report, but his job as a reporter was to discern the most important ones, the ones which revealed who Jesus actually was and what his mission was on the earth.

It didn't take him long to discover that the Son of God was in none of the expected places. So he winged his way to Capernaum and Bethsaida, then circled the Sea of Galilee. To his surprise, it was in an obscure little village in Galilee called Cana that he found his Lord. But even more surprising to him was what Jesus was doing: after all that stringent fasting in the desert, he was feasting at a wedding, talking to a group of men who appeared to be fascinated by what he was saying. There was music, there was dancing, there was abundant food and plenty of wine. Judging by the semi-recumbent postures of numerous guests, the wedding feast had been going on for a long, long time. There was more than gaiety amongst some of the groups, there was raucousness. Raphael avoided those groups, choosing, instead, to hover above his Lord and Master as he listened carefully to what he was saying to the more sober of the wedding guests.

But who was this lovely woman hurrying towards him? Raphael looked more closely, smiling when he recognised Mary. She had been beautiful as a young girl, but even now, being a good deal older than when he had last seen her, Raphael observed that her beauty had not faded. Her face, although puckered a little in some mild domestic worry, still had that humble, obedient expression he had noted when he had first laid his eyes on her. Some of that youthful innocence had matured to what appeared to be a deep-seated contentment and her gait was now more confident and assured, but she was still the most appealing woman Raphael had ever seen; it was her graceful serenity that made her face and her gestures stand out amongst the other women at the wedding feast. Raphael would go so far as to say that she outshone the bride, despite her more modest attire and the simplicity of her blue and white robe.

She reached the place where Jesus was reclining as he discoursed among the male guests. She didn't interrupt him though. Politely, she stood near him, waiting patiently for him to notice her. Jesus looked at her directly and said: "Mother, what is it? You are concerned about something?"

"My son," she said calmly, "they have run out of wine."

"Why do you bother me now," he replied, not unkindly. "My time has not yet come." (John 2 v 4)

Mary smiled knowingly, but she left him and went straight to some of the servants who were gesticulating to each other and wondering what they were going to do. Meanwhile, the bridegroom was saying to his own mother, "We will be disgraced. Our hospitality will be called into question. How on earth could we have predicted that so many extra guests would come to our wedding feast."

"You and your wife are loved by the villagers. They all want to celebrate with you." His mother tried to encourage him. But instead of making him happy, her words seemed to cast him into the deepest gloom. "But mother," he said as he frowned and twisted his fine wedding robe in frustration, creasing it in the process, "what is a wedding without wine!"

"What indeed! But there is nothing we can do about that now. It is too late to order in extra supplies. Your guests will just have to be satisfied with water. We are, after all, in the advanced stages of the feast. Perhaps your guests will not notice." She paused, looking around, then added wryly, "Indeed, some of them will be too drunk to notice. So don't worry. Go and enjoy your bride." It was at this point that something so extraordinary happened that Raphael knew that he was in the right place at the right time. Having carefully noted every word and action of both Jesus' mother, his Lord himself, the servants and the master of the banquet, he couldn't wait to pen his next article for *The Heavenly Chronicle* so that his words could be trumpeted across the heavens.

Chapter Ten

Before he took up his stylus to write on the large papyrus scroll that had been provided for him, Raphael meditated on the significance of the event he had just witnessed. Clearly, what had happened was an awesome display of the power of God; no human on earth could ever perform such a miraculous feat. In the natural scheme of things, changing water into wine was impossible. True, there might be some tricksters who could pretend to change water into wine; those fake magicians who could drop a substance into the water to make it appear red or who could actually substitute the ceremonial water jars for wineskins at the last minute (although the servants carrying away the water jars would have to be mightily quick about it to avoid detection). But nobody, not even a priest, a king or the most powerful magician in the world, could succeed in actually changing water into wine – unless this man happened to be the Son of God himself, for whom, like his father, nothing was impossible. Surely men were now going to open their eyes and understand with their hearts about who Jesus was? What a privilege for them that God had chosen to send his own son to live amongst them, and that Jesus had been willing to submit himself to his father's plan for the world. It must have been incredibly hard for him to separate himself so obediently from the presence of God.

Raphael wanted to report what had happened as accurately as possible so that the angels in heaven could also celebrate Jesus' glory. So, sitting down on his cloud cushion, he took up his writing equipment and began his article. When he had finished, two angel trumpeters fetched it and immediately began to announce the news, line by line, to every corner of the heavens.

Jesus Changes water into wine

In the late afternoon at a wedding in the small village of Cana, Galilee, Jesus performed an amazing miracle.

The bridegroom, despite having prepared well for his wedding feast, had not been expecting so many guests at the celebration of his marriage to his lovely new bride. So even though the wedding banquet was at an advanced stage, he was extremely perturbed when the wine ran out. By all the Jesus replied, "Dear woman, why do you rules of hospitality in Israel, he had failed in his obligations as a host, a serious shortfall and one for which he felt disgraced.

But Jesus' mother, Mary, noticed the bridegroom's consternation.

Obviously wanting to redeem this man in the eyes of his guests, and so that the celebrations could continue unabated, she approached her son and said, "They have no more wine."

100

involve me? My time has not yet come." (John 2 v 4)

Respectfully, Mary left her son, but with a knowing smile, she went over to the servants and said, "Do whatever he tells you." (2 John v 5)

So the servants stood near to Jesus, waiting for his instructions. Jesus stood up, and with calm authority, he pointed to the six stone water jars nearby, the ones that the Jews used for ceremonial washing. He told them to fill the jars with water. They followed his instructions to the letter, filling each jar to its very brim.

Jesus then looked up to heaven; his lips were moving, as if he was uttering a silent prayer to his father. After this, he turned to the servants and said, "Now draw some out and take it to the master of the banquet." (John 2 v 8) The servants obediently drew some of the liquid and took it straight to the master of the banquet to taste. The man smelt the liquid, swirled it around in his mouth as he savoured it, then instructed the servants to call over the bridegroom.

With a frown on his face, clearly expecting to be reprimanded, the bridegroom went to hear what the master of the banquet had to say. But instead of looking ashamed, the bridegroom's face broke into a broad smile at the master's words: "Everyone brings out the choice wine first and then the cheaper wine after the guests have had too much to drink; but you have saved the best till now." (John 2 v 10)

When Jesus' disciples drank some of this "water" that he had changed into wine, they were clearly astonished. They began to talk among themselves, many of them saying, with amazement, "Could this possibly be the Messiah that the prophets spoke about?

Who else could possibly do such an extraordinary miracle?" And so at that wedding in Cana of Galilee, the Christ revealed his glory not only to his disciples, but also to anyone else who was prepared to see, listen and understand.

Raphael
The Heavenly Chronicle

Before the last trumpet sound had even blared out the good news across the heavens or the last wispy letter had been written in the clouds, the members of the heavenly orchestra had already started tuning their instruments. Thousands upon thousands of violinists were massing to the huge amphitheatre where, apart from the ones in the throne room itself, the most significant celebrations were observed. The trumpeters, players of brass instruments and percussionists had already arrived and the harpists, who had a permanent enclave at the entrance to the auditorium, were melodiously plucking their strings, creating uplifting but rather soothing music as a prelude to the grander sounds that would soon be echoing across the skies. The choirs flew in last of all, excitedly chattering as they took their places on the stands, obviously thrilled to be singing out the praises of the Son of God. The creators of the worshipful lyrics for these occasions had speedily composed a new song, specifically to honour Jesus' miracle of changing so much ordinary water into so much fine wine, and to proclaim the significance of this event to every single angel who formed part of the heavenly host.

Above the earth where Raphael was hovering, some strains of this exquisite music reached his ears; he felt pleased that a celebration was about to occur, but also a little saddened that he couldn't be right there adoring his Lord and his God in the midst of that multitude of heavenly worshippers.

Just as the thought crossed his mind, he was aware of a mighty wind above him; he looked over his shoulder to see a group of angels speeding towards him. This looked serious. What emergency had occurred now! He hoped it wasn't another rebellion against the Lord of the universe, and that he, Raphael, a peace-loving angel, was not going to be asked to fight in a celestial war. He turned completely around to face the approaching messengers from heaven, ready to receive his instructions and prepared to carry them out exactly as directed.

As they got closer, he was surprised to see that Gideon was not amongst this group. But he smiled as he remembered that one of this angel's favourite pursuits was to direct celebratory massed choirs. How could he have forgotten! As one of the chief countertenors in the celestial choir of angels, he had been directed often enough by Gideon… he loved the choir master's flair and style. But most of all, he appreciated the encouragement and the constructive criticism that this knowledgeable angel gave to each member of that massive choir. He would spend hours working with individual angels through their parts in song after song and hymn after hymn. Above all, Gideon loved to give glory to God and to his son; he considered it an incredible privilege to guide every single angel to celestial singing excellence. Perfect harmonies from humble and adoring hearts were the only appropriate responses for the King and Lord of the universe, the one who had created all things. How Raphael had enjoyed standing in the midst of that celestial choir as the sweet sounds of his countertenor voice blended in with the rest of the singers in beautiful harmonies. Raphael was shaken out of his reverie by the rich, deep voice of Gabriel, the chief messenger.

"Michael has sent me to fetch you," he said. Raphael experienced a vivid flashback to the violence of the war in heaven that had resulted in Lucifer and his rebellious angels being thrown out of God's heavenly kingdom. The flaming swords that Michael and his warrior angels had used and the dedication and commitment of his troops of holy angels were no match for Satan and his evil minions who had skulked off to the earthly realms where they were spitefully causing havoc.

Raphael had not shirked in his duty and had fought bravely in that battle, but it had taken its toll on him, both physically and mentally. He waited anxiously for the announcement about the next battle. But to his great relief, it did not come. Instead, Gabriel had good news for him.

"The Lord thinks you deserve to be celebrating with all the other angels. Because Jesus has shown his glory to mankind and his disciples' faith in him, all heaven is partying... and Michael feels that you would make a great contribution to the choir."

"But what about my work here?"

"Admittedly, this will just be a brief respite from your work on earth. You will not be participating in the extended celebration as some of the other angels will be doing. But you are not going to miss out entirely, even though your presence in heaven will be brief. So you are free to come with us."

"Thank you, thank you."

"Don't thank me – I'm just the messenger, as you are well aware. Thank the Lord of the universe."

"You are so right. Holy Lord God of heaven and earth, I praise you and I thank you that you have chosen to include me in this wonderful celebration to honour your son. In recognition of who he is, your only son, and in acknowledgement of what he is able to do, mighty miracles, I will use the gifts you have given me to sing joyfully, so that the whole of heaven will praise and honour and worship and glorify you."

"Now, follow us and we'll take you to the very heart of the festivities."

Raphael felt his spirits lift as he winged his way, once again, from the earth into the very heart of heaven. He was going to enjoy every single moment of the brief period that had been allocated to him to praise the Lord with thousands upon thousands of other angels. After that, he was confident that his spirit would be refreshed; he would then be able to continue with his job as a chronicler with renewed enthusiasm.

Chapter Eleven

As Raphael soared towards his heavenly home, he felt so elated that he lifted his voice in adoration to the amazing God of the universe. What a privilege it was for him to be joining in this wonderful celebration. If only the saints on earth could even have an inkling of how special, varied and glorious it was to be surrounded by multitudes of fellow worshippers – archangels, angels, elders, saints from every tribe and every nation – all glorifying God with instruments, songs, hymns and dances – but most strikingly, with their whole beings.

The outward signs of their active worship were pretty impressive: the exultant flinging of arms in the air, the excited abandonment with which the dancers moved their feet, the frenetic clapping of their hands, the respectful bowing of their heads, knees and bodies, even to the extent of prostrating themselves before the infinite, powerful, mighty, unsearchable God of the whole universe who had created all things. But all these shows of adoration for their God paled into insignificance in comparison with what the archangels, angels, elders and saints were feeling in their inner beings as they grasped with their minds and experienced with their hearts who exactly they were worshipping. Because all the worship in the world and across the whole of the heavens couldn't possibly do justice to the Almighty God who had created all things in their exquisite complexity and variety.

It was not unusual to see an elder or a saint falling to his knees, crying out in a loud voice or even welling up with tears of adoration. So moving and inspiring were these wonderful celebrations, and so omnipotent, mighty and unsearchable was the God whom they all worshipped that it was impossible not to be deeply moved by these occasions. And being in God's very presence was such a sublime encounter that Raphael felt totally unable to describe his experiences and feelings in a manner that would do them justice. He just wished everyone in the heavens above and on the earth below could feel just what he was feeling right now. Then there would be no more discontentment, no more violence, no more evil. He longed for the day that sin would be completely eradicated so that everyone could live in peace and harmony once more, praising the God of heaven and worshipping his son.

Even when he was still a long way off, Raphael, whose ear had always been eagerly tuned to the different types of choral voices, could hear the pure sound of the sopranos, the varied colour of the mezzo-sopranos, especially the coloraturas and the dramatic voices of the contraltos. But it was the male voices that lifted his spirits the most: he began humming as he anticipated joining in with the celestial choir that at that very moment was filling the heavens with uplifting songs of praise as they glorified their God and their king for his marvellous deeds and his wondrous works. The richness of the tenors, the heavy sounds of the baritones and the deep strong voices of the bases blended beautifully with the sweet smoothness of the countertenor voices. Raphael enjoyed his role as a countertenor: he and his fellow countertenors added a touch of uniqueness to the heavenly choirs. Because their voices were rare, they were like precious gems sewn in to the tapestry of the already magnificent choirs of angels. Not that he was a proud angel: it was just that he loved to be able to contribute something special to the already perfect harmonies of the heavenly choirs.

Just as Raphael arrived at the spacious arena, there was a loud blast from the trumpeters. Although the blast of the trumpeters was not specifically designed for announcing his particular arrival in the heavenly realms, he praised God in his heart for the impressiveness of his welcome. He heard a tuning of instruments, followed by a clash of cymbals and a roll of drums, then every singer in the celestial choir lifted his voice in adoration, singing a new song that was inspired by the amazing miracle that Jesus had just performed on earth in the small village of Cana in Galilee:

"Sing a new song to our glorious God
Sending his son to the earth.
Showing his glory, displaying his power
Changing the water to wine.
Chorus
Praise our King, hail our God, praise our glorious Lord,
He is matchless in might and in power.
Praise our King, hail our God, Hallelujah to Him,
He is gracious, abounding in love.

Show all the world he is worthy of praise

Honour and worship and awe.
Teaching mankind about Jesus his son
Proving that he is the Lord.
Chorus
Praise our King, hail our God, praise our glorious Lord,
He is matchless in might and in power.
Praise our King, hail our God, Hallelujah to him,
He is gracious, abounding in love.

Opening the eyes of rebellious man,
Revealing his glory on earth.
Powerful miracles used to display
God who has come to the earth.
Chorus
Praise our King, hail our God, praise our glorious Lord,
He is matchless in might and in power.
Praise our King, hail our God, hallelujah to him,
He is gracious, abounding in love.

Changing the water to wine shows his power,
Majesty, glory and might.
Making a way for his followers now
To believe and to trust in the Christ.
Chorus
Praise our King, hail our God, praise our glorious Lord,
He is matchless in might and in power.
Praise our King, hail our God, hallelujah to him,
He is gracious, abounding in love."

With great joy in his heart and with humble adoration, Raphael joined the multitudinous choirs of angels as they sang this new song to their Lord and King, celebrating his might, his miraculous power, but most of all his grace. What a privilege to have actually witnessed the miracle at firsthand, to have relayed the news to the heavenly hosts and to be singing with them now, praising and honouring and glorifying God.

But this was just the first of many uplifting celebrations. If he was to observe the Son of Man's every move on earth, he knew he would be reporting on numerous extraordinary miracles and events taking place on the earth in and around Galilee and Judea. He was excited to be used by God, as a humble instrument who was willing to be a small part of God's plan to reveal his glory both on earth and in the heavenly realms.

Chapter Twelve

As soon as he had travelled back to earth, Raphael was amazed to see how many people were following Jesus around wherever he went. The minute he entered a town, the people flocked to him; if he went to the countryside to get away from the crowds so that he could pray to his father, the people followed him there too. Sometimes, the crush of the crowd pressing in on him was so overpowering that he got into a boat with his disciples and was pushed off from the shore so that he could teach them more effectively. Clearly, he loved teaching, and obviously, both men and women loved listening to him. And even when he looked tired, he never flagged from sharing the good news about God and his kingdom with anybody who was prepared to listen.

Early one morning, after Jesus had been praying on a Galilean mountainside, Raphael noticed that a man was staring upwards, obsessively watching every step that Jesus took as he descended the mountain. Clearly, he was waiting for Jesus. Unusually, there were no large crowds who normally followed Jesus everywhere. On closer inspection, Raphael understood why. This man who was so anxiously staring towards Jesus was deformed. On the hand that he stretched towards the Master, the fingers were shrivelled – eaten away, and his other arm was a stump. As Jesus got closer and the man stumbled towards him, Raphael noticed that he also had a bad limp. One leg was clearly much shorter than the other. But it was the man's face that was the most disturbing part of his body: it looked as if an animal had bitten off part of his nose, his chin and cheeks were receding badly, as if chunks of flesh had been torn out by a wild animal, and he only appeared to have one ear. Obviously, nobody wanted to go anywhere near this grossly disfigured man. As a leper, he was a complete outcast from society. Even more tragically, being in an advanced state of leprosy, this horrific and painful dreaded disease which ate away every part of the body, this man was left by the community to die – an agonising and lonely death.

Raphael couldn't help feeling sorry for this sick man, this outcast, this 'unclean' person. He had seen how the community and the religious leaders, particularly the Pharisees, treated people of his ilk. They wanted nothing to do with people like that: according to them, that kind of man could pollute them, not only physically, but spiritually as well. But Jesus did not shun this man as everybody else had. Instead, he walked straight towards the man. Raphael watched with baited breath as the leper fell with his face to the ground in front of Jesus. Then, slightly lifting his head from his prostrate position, the leper, with a wavering voice, said: "Lord, if you are willing, you can make me clean." (Luke 5 v 12)

Then Raphael, from his position above the earth, saw something remarkable. Without hesitation, Jesus did something that was unheard of for men to do – unthinkable –

looking at the man with great compassion, he actually reached out and touched the man's deformed arm.

Raphael noticed a shiver of anticipation in what was left of the man's body. The human touch! Something he obviously hadn't experienced for a very long time! The precious touch of another man's hand on his wasted body. And the touch of a whole, clean man! That made what had just happened even more special. Jesus looked directly at the man, held his broken arm firmly and said, in a voice filled with compassion, "I am willing. Be clean!" (Luke 5 v 13) Before Raphael's very eyes, at that very instant, an amazing transformation occurred. The man stood up on his legs, raised his healed arms to the sky, then ran his hands over his nose, his cheeks, his chin. He was so stunned by what had happened to him that he was utterly silent for a while. All the leprosy was gone! Instead of sores and holes, his whole body was completely restored.

Then Raphael heard Jesus' calm, reassuring voice giving the man instructions, but the ex-leper was already walking away, raising his arms and shouting, "I am clean. I am clean."

Raphael was excited by what he had just witnessed. He knew that yet again, this amazing, newsworthy event, this miraculous healing, must be reported as soon as possible in *The Heavenly Chronicle.* The heavenly hosts needed to give glory and honour to their compassionate, glorious king.

But before he could even begin writing his article, he noticed a group of men hurrying towards Jesus. Judging from their attire, they looked like Jewish elders. At their head, was a confident man who, judging by his position in the group, the most influential person there.

Someone in the crowd murmured, "The centurion's servant is approaching the Master." A centurion's servant! Roman centurions were secretly spurned by the Jewish people, especially by the Zealots who wanted nothing to do with the Roman occupying forces! In fact, they were awaiting a Messiah who could lead a rebellion and overthrow the hated occupiers. There were exceptions, of course, like some of the Romans who respected the Jewish traditions. Like this man and his servant?

When the man caught up with Jesus, he said to him, "Master, in Capernaum lies my master's sick servant who is greatly valued by him. But this servant is paralysed and in terrible pain. His condition is rapidly deteriorating – my master thinks he is going to die soon."

"Sir," said a nearby elder, "this man deserves to have his servant healed. He loves our nation and has built our synagogue. (Luke 7 v 4) He sent us to fetch you."

Immediately, Jesus said to the elders: "I will go and heal the man's servant."

Raphael watched him going with the group. But while they were on the way, he saw a group of what looked like servants hurrying to Jesus. Their spokesperson cried out, "Sir, our master sent us to find you. This is what he instructed me to say to you as soon as I found you." He took a deep breath and then went about reciting the words his master had given him to say: "Teacher, don't trouble yourself to go all that way. I myself am a man of authority. When I tell my staff, do this, they do it. So if you, as a man of authority, just say the word, I know that my servant will be healed." Jesus looked around at the assembled gathering. "I tell you," he said, "I have not found such great faith even in Israel." (Luke 7 v 9) Then he turned to the centurion's servant and said in a loud, clear voice so that everyone there could hear, "Go! It will be done just as you believed it would."

Raphael overheard some servants talking later that day. He discovered that the centurion's servant had been healed at the exact time that Jesus had spoken those words. Now, it was definitely time to pen another article for *The Heavenly Chronicle*. He winged his way to the cloud sanctuary he used as his office, lifted the golden stylus from its sheath and in bold strokes, he engraved his article across the sky so his message could be picked up by the trumpeters and broadcast across the heavens.

Jesus miraculously restores sick men to complete health

Early one morning, Jesus was coming down from a mountainside in Galilee where he had been praying to his father. Although the usual crowds weren't at the bottom of the mountain to greet him, there was one man who had been patiently waiting for him: an 'unclean' man, a leper, scorned by the people and forbidden to enter the temple or even the towns.

A lonely, desperate and very sick man, suffering greatly from this destructive disease which had literally eaten into many parts of his body, including his face, arms, hands, legs and feet, he threw himself at Jesus' feet and cried out, "Lord, if you are willing, you can make me clean." (Luke 5 v 12) Jesus reached out his hand and touched what was left of the man's arm, saying in a calm, clear voice, "I am willing. Be clean." (Luke 5 v 13) At that very moment, a remarkable thing happened. The man stood up on his restored legs, raised his now complete arms above his head in a joyful gesture, then felt his face. "I am clean! I am clean!" he cried, actually jumping for joy. But while he was in the midst of his elation, Jesus firmly warned him: "Don't tell anyone what has happened to you. But go, show yourself to the priests and offer the sacrifices that Moses commanded for your cleansing, as a testimony to them." (Luke 5 v 14)

The man, however, could not restrain himself. He excitedly told everyone he saw how Jesus had healed him of his leprosy. This resulted in Jesus being mobbed wherever he went. Instead of staying inside the towns, he had to stay on the outskirts so that he could continue to teach his disciples. But thousands of men, women and children, especially the sick among them, searched for him, found him and followed him everywhere.

It was on one of these occasions that Jesus performed another amazing miracle. This time, it wasn't a weak, vulnerable man who approached him, but some Jewish elders went with the centurion's servant to find Jesus. Although his master, a centurion, was one of the hated of the occupying Roman forces, he was tolerated by the Jews and even admired by some of them. That is why the Jewish elders had consented to take his message.

"Sir," the chief elder said to Jesus, "a centurion asks that you heal his sick, paralysed, faithful servant who lies dying at his home."

"Sir," added another elder, "this man deserves to have you

heal his servant. He built our synagogue and he shows respect for our nation." Immediately, Jesus turned around to follow the group of elders. "I will come with you to heal this sick man," he said.

But as they got closer to the town, another group of men came running along the road to meet Jesus. "Teacher," said their spokesperson, "our master says that you mustn't go into his house. He says he does not deserve that."

Another servant continued: "He said I must tell you... he is a man of authority. He tells one of us, do this, and we do it. He says to his soldiers, 'Do that', and they obey him. So he told me to say... 'Just say the word, and my servant will be healed'." (Matthew 8 v 8)

Jesus looked around at the gathering crowds and said, "I tell you the truth. I have not found anyone in Israel with such great faith." (Luke 8 v 10) To the centurion's servant he said, "Your master's servant is healed."

"Thank you," he said, glancing up at the sky as he hurried to his master's home, muttering, "Mid-morning."

But on the way to the centurion's home, this group was met with some more servants – however, these men were not sad; in fact, they were the opposite: they were rejoicing. "Our fellow servant is well," explained one of them. "His illness has left him. He is completely restored to health."

"Hallelujah, glory to God," shouted some of the surrounding people.

When the servant got home and saw that his colleague was well again, he was very glad. His master met him and rejoiced with him. "My faithful servant was made well again. At mid-morning, his illness left him completely! What happened?"

"Mid-morning," smiled his servant. "That is exactly the time the teacher said he would be well again."

"Praise God," cried the centurion. "Jesus has healed my servant just as I knew he would. What a great miracle."

Once again, the Son of God is stamping his authority on earth and proving his divinity for those humans who have eyes to see.

Raphael
The Heavenly Chronicle

When the good news about these amazing healings were trumpeted through the clouds, the angels assembled once again to give due homage to the King of Kings and Lord of Lords. Their praises resounded from one end of the heavens to the other.

For Raphael, all the events that he had already witnessed on earth that were associated with his Lord's power and compassion made him feel in a constant celebratory mood. While he was disappointed to note the opposition Jesus was receiving from the sons of men, and could not quite understand it, every time his Lord displayed his power and authority on earth, Raphael wanted to trumpet the news from one end of the earth to the other. If only he could shake the sons of men and wake them up from their selfish stupor. But he knew that was not his mission: he had been sent to chronicle Jesus' walk on earth so that the good news that was unfolding could be celebrated in the heavens. And he was certainly continually being surprised by the awesome events he was witnessing.

But it wasn't only the spectacular miracles that touched his heart. It was also the quieter moments that Jesus had with individuals that accentuated for Raphael just how compassionate, caring and gracious God's son was.

One day, as Jesus was travelling from Judea to Galilee, his journey brought him to Sychar, a small town in Samaria which was close to a plot of ground Jacob had given to his son, Joseph. It was the sixth hour, and the day was already beginning to feel hot; Jesus was clearly tired after his travels, so he sat down by Jacob's well while his disciples went into the town to buy food.

Raphael, who by now had a good idea about the culture and habits of the men he had been observing, was very surprised by what transpired next. He noticed that one of the Samaritan women from the town had come to draw water. To his amazement, Jesus began to talk to her; even she was surprised, as men, especially Jewish men, did not normally talk to, and in some cases even deign to associate, with women, especially Samaritans.

Raphael drew closer and hovered just above their heads in order to hear the conversation more clearly. The woman did look up as the wind from his wing passed over her face, which made Raphael retract slightly just in case he could be seen, but to his relief, she brushed her face with her hand and stared at Jesus as he asked her: "Will you give me a drink?"

She did looked startled, but she decided to clear the air by asking a question of her own: "You are a Jew and I am a Samaritan woman. How can you ask me for a drink?"

That thought had crossed Raphael's mind too, but he was beginning to realise that his Lord and God was full of surprises, and that he was constantly smashing stereotypes. Jesus replied, "If you knew the gift of God and who it is that asks you for a drink, you would have asked him and he would have given you living water."(John 4 v 10)

By this time, Raphael's emotions had been thoroughly stirred. He was incredibly moved by the fact that the King of the universe, his Lord and God, was patiently explaining to this insignificant, ostracised Samaritan woman – albeit in symbols and riddles – about the precious gift of true life.

Puzzled and taking what Jesus had said to her literally, she replied, "Sir, you have nothing to draw water with and the well is deep. Where can you get this living water? Are you greater than our father Jacob, who gave us this well and drank from it himself, as did also his sons and his flocks and herds?" (John 4 vs 11-12)

Jesus' inspiring reply lifted Raphael's spirits. "Everyone who drinks from this water," said Jesus, "will be thirsty again, but whoever drinks the water I give him will never thirst. Indeed, the water I give him will become in him a spring of water welling up to eternal life." (John 14 v 13)

Jesus' profound words were still misunderstood by this humble Samaritan woman who was continuing to take his words literally. "Sir," she replied, "give me this water so that I won't get thirsty and have to keep coming here to draw water."

Raphael wasn't expecting Jesus' next command and nor was the woman: "Go, call your husband and come back."

She immediately responded, "I have no husband."

Jesus' next remark proved that he had deep insight into her life and that he was no ordinary man: "You are right when you say you have no husband. The fact is, you have had five husbands, and the man you now have is not your husband. What you have just said is quite true."

At last, the woman realised that the man she was talking to was special in some way: "I can see that you are a prophet," she said. "Our fathers worshipped on this mountain, but the Jews say it is right to worship in Jerusalem."

"A time is coming when you will worship the Father neither on this mountain nor in Jerusalem... salvation is from the Jews... the true worshippers will worship the father in spirit and truth, for they are the kind of worshippers the father seeks. God is spirit, and his worshippers must worship in spirit and in truth." (John 4 vs 21-24)

The woman was getting closer to the truth when she said: "I know the Messiah – called the Christ – is coming. When he comes, he will explain everything to us."

Jesus' next words galvanised the woman: "I who speak to you am he." (John 4 v 26) Immediately, she ran into town and got as many of her friends and relatives as she could to come out and meet the Messiah.

While she was gathering some followers, the disciples came back to Jesus with food. The Lord took advantage of the situation to give these men an object lesson: "I have food to eat that you know nothing about." (John 4 v 32) When they expressed their confusion, he graciously explained further: "My food is to do the will of him who sent me and to finish his work." (John 4 v 34)

Before the disciples had time to absorb what Jesus was saying to them, he was approached by the woman and all the people she had managed to gather. They persuaded him to stay with them for two days, and so he patiently taught them and explained to them how they should be living, as well as unpacking to them his own mission on earth and how they could be saved.

Raphael felt that it was an incredible privilege for him to be observing the Son of God in such close proximity as he moved among the sons of men; and he was deeply conscious of the responsibility he had been given to relay the news across the heavens so that the angels, saints and all the other celestial beings could rejoice as they exalted and worshipped with ever-increasing intensity the King of King and Lord of Lords.

What Raphael had just witnessed – the conversion, or at least potential conversion, of a whole village of Samaritan citizens – was something worth broadcasting to the celestial world. So he didn't waste time getting his stylus and composing the first words of the article that would be triumphant in tone and inspiring in content.

Village of Samaritans converted by Christ

An extraordinary miracle took place in the small Samaritan village of Sychar near Jacob's well. This wasn't a healing of the body but a life-changing restoration of a woman's heart and soul, which resulted in many conversions in what the Jews thought was an insignificant place.

At the sixth hour, after a long journey from Judea, Jesus and his disciples had to pass through Samaria on their way to Galilee. It was there, in the tiny village of Sychar, that Jesus met with a Samaritan woman in an encounter that was to change her life.

His disciples had gone into town to buy some

food. As Jesus was tired, he sat down by Jacob's well. When he saw a Samaritan woman drawing water from the well, breaking with tradition (as it was the custom for Jews not to talk directly to strange women, and especially not to Samaritan women who were considered to be impure), he asked her to give him a drink. She was so surprised to have been addressed by a Jewish man that she expressed her reservations immediately, asking him how he, as a Jew who did not associate with her kind, could possibly be asking her for a drink.

It was at this point that Jesus took the opportunity to teach her some life-changing truths. She did not understand what he was saying to her at the beginning, but he patiently persisted in proving to her who he was and what he could offer her.

He spoke to her of 'living water', the type of water that restores the soul and leads to eternal life. Puzzled, she asked him where he could get this 'living water', as he had nothing with which to draw water and the well was deep. It was then that the Son of God offered her his gift of life: "Everyone who drinks this water," he explained, "will be thirsty again, but whoever drinks the water I give him will never thirst. Indeed, the water I give him will become in him a spring of water welling up to eternal life." (John 4 vs 13-14)

Of course she wanted that water then, but still, she didn't understand the significance of what Jesus was offering her. "Sir," she replied, "give me this water so that I won't get thirsty and have to keep coming here to draw water." (John 4 v 15) Instead of displaying impatience because of her failure to understand, Jesus calmly asked her to call her husband. When she said that she had no husband, the Christ demonstrated that he knew so much more about her than she realised. He told her some home truths about her having had five husbands, and the man living with her was not her husband.

So amazed was she that she called him a prophet and began to talk about her ancestors worshipping on the mountain nearby Sychar; however she seemed confused that the Jews stated that the only place to worship was in the temple at Jerusalem.

Jesus' reply was profound: "...true worshippers will worship the father in spirit and truth, for they are the kind of worshippers the Father seeks. God is spirit and his worshippers must worship in spirit and in

Raphael
The Heavenly Chronicle

truth." (John 4 vs 23-24)

At this point, I sensed that the scales were gradually beginning to drop off this woman's eyes, especially when she said: "I know that Messiah (called Christ) is coming. When he comes, he will explain everything to us." (John 4 v 25)

I could see the light dawning in her eyes at Jesus' next words: "I who speak to you am he." (John 4 v 26) Wonderfully though, she followed up her belief with action and went to call the villagers to come and see the Messiah. Jesus was persuaded to stay with them for two days; days in which he took every opportunity to explain the word of God to them.

Hallelujah! It is time to rejoice when the sons of men believe that Jesus was sent to earth to reveal the true God, his father, to them.

This time, the sung praises and the 'Hallelujas' of the angels were so loud that they even reached an obscure corner of Israel where a little girl and her mother were praying that the Messiah would come to save his people. Fortunately, Raphael was there to witness this touching incident. Not wanting to miss any of Jesus' miracles or his profound words, and also wanting to see what reaction his marvellous works and wonderful parables were having on the people, he decided to flit around from one ordinary home to another, gathering information as he went.

It was on one of these fact-finding missions that he had come across a small girl and her mother praying on the roof of their home. This might not be as spectacular as the celebrations that were going on at that very moment in heaven, but the child's faith and the mother's sincerity were just as honouring to God. As Raphael listened carefully to the exchange between mother and child, he could feel his spirits lifting. He was left with a strong desire to dance, even though he knew this would disturb the air above them and hint at his presence.

Chapter Thirteen

"That was a beautiful prayer, Joanna," Raphael overheard the young mother saying to her daughter.

"Thank you, Mother," said the little girl excitedly. "Can we thank God for the stars in the sky, and the big bright moon, and the sun, and… "

"Of course we can," replied the mother. "Let's pray together."

"God, thank you for the stars in the sky," said the little girl.

"Amen," responded her mother.

"And God, thank you for the beautiful moon."

"Amen. Glory be to the God of heaven."

"And God, thank you for the big, bright sun."

"Thank you Lord. Praise to your glorious name."

Now it was the little girl's turn to say, "Amen. Amen," which she did with great enthusiasm.

"And thank you that Peter went to Jesus to ask for the healing of his mother-in-law."

"Thank you God for making Bube better."

"Amen. Amen," said the mother.

"Amen. Amen. Amen," chorused the little girl.

"God is good," said the mother, followed by the little girl's excited repetition.

"God is great," said the mother.

This time when the little girl repeated what her mother had said, she clapped her hands.

"God is holy."

The girl's high-pitched, eager response was full of joy.

Then, quite suddenly, the little girl put her finger to her lips and, listening intently, looked up at the sky. The mother, in mid-praise-sentence, turned to her daughter, saying anxiously, "What is it, Joanna?"

"Mother, did you hear that?" she replied in a voice that was little above a whisper.

The mother's expression changed to a slight frown as she said, slowly and deliberately, "Joanna dearest, I didn't hear anything."

"But listen, Mummy. Listen." Then once again, the small child put her finger to her lips and looked up at the sky.

Raphael continued to hover, trying not to disturb the air above their heads. But he did smile as he heard the sound of more than a thousand violins tuning. The angelic orchestra was getting ready to fill the whole of heaven with their exquisite harmonies.

"It's just the wind," shrugged the mother. But she hesitated, as if she was about to change her mind. "A strong, sweet wind… like thousands of rustling leaves – I've never heard a wind like that –"

"It's not a wind," insisted the little girl, "it's… "

"Oh, Joanna," replied the mother, slightly impatiently. "It must be the wind – a beautiful wind, but a wind all the same."

Joanna shook her head gravely. "It sounds like... when we're outside the temple and we can hear them making music inside."

The mother concentrated on the sound. "Oh Joanna, you're right. It sounds like violins... and trumpets... and... I think I can hear a harp." She looked around. "But that's impossible. There's no orchestra here." She scratched her head.

Although the sound of the celestial orchestra playing was distant – like faint background music – it was quite distinct. Raphael, like this mother, could clearly distinguish the sounds of the violin players from those of the trumpeters and the harpists. At that moment, he so badly wanted to celebrate with the heavenly orchestra and choir. As the mother was doing, he listened intently to the enthusiastic praise songs that the heavenly choirs were singing. Of course, he had an advantage over Joanna and her mother. He had been there, he had heard the orchestra and the choirs at firsthand; more than that, he himself had participated in these glorious celebrations, honouring God to the best of his ability as he lifted his voice in adoration. He even knew exactly what they were playing and singing: "Holy, holy, holy is the Lord God Almighty. The whole earth is full of his glory."

How wonderful that this distant worship had travelled through the air all the way to the earth. For that to happen, Raphael knew that the full complement of choirs had joined in on this joyful occasion. Nobody had been left out, so the sound was richer and more intensely passionate than usual; it also had much more volume, which was why the melodious praise could be heard so far away, even by some humans. For a moment, Raphael closed his eyes and luxuriated in the exquisitely pure harmonies flowing from the heavens above.

So absorbed was Raphael by this lovely music that he didn't at first notice the large crowd surging forward towards the edge of the lake where Jesus was talking to his disciples. He also hadn't noticed that Joanna, holding tightly onto her mother's arm, had run forward to see what was going on. For her, all thoughts of music were now forgotten as she pulled her mother towards the crowd at the lake. When Raphael did open his eyes, he realised that something dramatic was bound to happen, so he flew close to the scene, straining to hear what Jesus was saying. He sympathised when he heard Jesus' words: "Let's go to the other side of the lake." From the urgency in his tone, Raphael could see that Jesus wanted to teach his followers something important. There was a time for healing the sick, but there was also a time for teaching his disciples important lessons about the kingdom of God. The disciples walked quickly with Jesus to Peter's boat. Once they were all seated, Peter pulled up the anchor and launched the boat into the water. Raphael, leaving Joanna, her mother and the crowds behind on the shore, decided to follow Jesus.

After a while, he saw him laying his head on his arm in the stern of the boat and closing his eyes. It gave him quite a jolt to see the Lord, the King of the Universe, looking so vulnerable. Yet as a man, experiencing all the weaknesses of the human body while he lived on the earth, clearly he needed rest from what must be his exhausting ministry of constant healing and teaching.

But one minute, his disciples were calm and relaxed, the next they were in a panic. What had happened, Raphael had come to know from observing the region closely, was common in this area. Quite often, because of its position in the hollow of the mountains, the Sea of Galilee could be like a millpond one minute, and like a wild, stormy ocean the next. Which was exactly what was happening now. A fierce wind had funnelled down from the mountains and was driving the water before it to create huge waves. It was these very waves that were crashing onto the deck while the violent wind was buffeting the boat this way and that. No wonder the disciples were in a panic. Many a fisherman had drowned in these waters. Raphael himself felt the need to help these men. But he stopped himself from plucking them one by one off the boat and transporting them through the air to the shore. Jesus was on that boat. And with Jesus on board, the men had no need to fear! He wished he could tell them that. Because these men were in sore need of encouragement. They looked absolutely terrified.

"Where's Jesus?" someone shouted.

The men were silent for a while as, holding desperately onto ropes and boards as the waves crashed over their heads, making them gasp for breath, they slowly – inch by inch – searched every plank of the vessel.

At last someone cried, "He's here. He's sleeping!"

This disciple proceeded to shake Jesus awake from his snatched slumber.

"Lord, Lord," cried this frantic discipline, "don't you care if we all drown."

130

Jesus looked compassionately at this man. Then, standing up, he raised his arms to the heavens.

"Wind. Be still," he commanded.

Instantly, the wind stopped howling.

"Waves. Stop crashing." Immediately, the waves died down and the sea was completely calm, like the millpond it had been when they set out. The men stared at Jesus in utter amazement. One of them said, "Who is this? Even the winds and the waves obey him!"

"What power!" cried another.

"He can only be from God."

"He is more than a prophet! He must be God. Nobody but God would have the power to command the winds and the waves to be still – and be instantly obeyed!"

"Hallelujah. The kingdom of God has come to the earth."

"Hallelujah. Hallelujah."

For the rest of the trip, the men became subdued. They stared at Jesus in wonder and awe. But Jesus sat calmly in their midst, a slight smile playing across his lips. Raphael could identify with that smile: Jesus had just been recognised for who he was – God come down to earth. What a wonderful revelation for these simple fishermen. Perhaps now they would follow him with more passion and commitment. And he would teach them more about who he really was.

But that teaching, Raphael saw, would have to wait. At the Gadarenes on the other side of the lake where the boat was heading, chaos had erupted. Jesus and his disciples were in for a rocky ride. Raphael, to his own regret, was feeling slightly anxious as he waited for events to unfold.

Chapter Fourteen

A wild, completely out-of-control man was running from the tombs cut into the hillside to meet Jesus. The man's very long, knotted hair streamed behind him, his unruly arms waved this way and that and what was left of his torn, tattered clothes barely covered his body. Some worried men who were close to the shore were watching this rough, ungovernable behaviour. One of them cried out a warning as Jesus stepped onto the shore: "Watch out. That man's violent."

"We've often put chains on his hands and feet, but it's no use. He snaps the chains as if they were frayed threads."

"No-one comes this way anymore," said another man. "It's dangerous. The only reason we're here is to keep watch – to see that he doesn't threaten our people."

"But he's bleeding!" remarked one of the disciples.

"That's because he's always cutting himself with sharp stones. He's crazy, this man. Get back in your boat."

"Yes. Stay away from him before he hurts you too."

Some of the disciples, looking really scared, were hovering near the boat, looking as if they were ready for a quick exit. But Jesus calmly stayed where he was, both of his feet planted firmly on the ground, even though the insane man was running straight for him, his cut and bleeding arms outstretched. At that moment, Raphael felt a strong urge to position himself in front of this crazy madman, but he managed to restrain himself. Of course, Jesus had the power to subdue this man. He was, after all, the Son of God! Feeling calmer, Raphael watched with fascination as the extraordinary event unfolded before him.

First, to Raphael's great surprise, this uncontrollable man propelled himself forward, landing on the ground at Jesus' feet. The disciple closest to Jesus looked with revulsion and fear at this bundle of untamed flesh.

Next, a cacophonous shriek issued from the man's mouth, causing two more of the disciples to step back from this monstrosity. Then, in a loud, clear voice, the 'man' looked up at Jesus, a tormented expression on his face: "What do you want with us, Son of God? Have you come to torture us before the appointed time?" (Matthew 8 v 29)

Evading the question, Jesus said simply, "What's your name?"

"Legion," came the shrieked reply, the sound threatening once again. "There are many, many of us." Then, in a more demanding voice: "Swear that you won't send us into the abyss – we don't want to go out of the area… send us into the pigs."

With authority, Jesus commanded, "Come out of this man you evil spirits. Go into the pigs."

At that very moment, the large herd of pigs – there looked as if there were two thousand of them – stampeded down the hill towards the lake. One after the other, they plunged into the water and didn't come up again.

The men nearby ran off to the village and brought back a crowd with them. In the meanwhile, Raphael had watched the 'wild man' clothe himself.

"How did this happen?" cried a villager, pointing to the man who had been restored to health. He was sitting at the feet of Jesus, clothed and in his right mind.

"Where are our pigs?" said another. "What will we have to live on now?"

"Please go away from here," said another man, pointing to Jesus.

"Right away from us...please go away now. We don't want you here."

"Please can I come with you," cried the man who had been healed by Jesus.

"No, you stay here and tell all the people how much God has done for you."

'Go away. Please," chorused the villagers. So Jesus got into the boat with his disciples and headed for the other side of the lake.

How could these people be so blind? Why were they not feting Jesus, celebrating the great miracle that had just been performed in front of their very eyes? Well, if earthly men weren't prepared to praise God for his remarkable power, Raphael knew that in heaven, yet another great celebration would occur the instant the angels heard what had just happened on earth. Because the angels never tired of praising God for the wondrous things that he had done and was continuing to do as he actively worked out his plan for humanity.

Raphael felt an urgent need to send news of Jesus' latest triumphs into the heavens. So with great enthusiasm, he went off to pen his article, humbly aware that he could never do justice to the mighty Lord and creator of the universe. But he would certainly try his best to record the events just as they had happened.

Jesus displays his power over the elements and drives out evil spirits

Early in the morning, the crowds were already gathering on the shore of the Sea of Galilee. They had followed Jesus there, and among them were many sickpeople. But Jesus, intent on teaching his disciples, instructed them to launch their boat so that they could find a quieter place on the other side.

When they left the shore, the sea was as calm as a millpond. Exhausted by his labours, Jesus fell sound asleep in the stern of the boat. But as is common in this part of the world, fierce winds funnelled down from the hills, black clouds built up above the sea and a furious storm broke out. Huge waves assaulted the disciples' boat, tossing it this way and that, so that every man there except Jesus, who was still sleeping, was terrified. Clinging desperately to ropes or rails, they shouted out to each other. One of them found Jesus sleeping and shook him awake.

"Teacher, don't you care if we drown?" (Mark 4 v 38) he accused.

Shaking himself from his slumber and sitting

up calmly, he said, "Where is your faith?"

Then, turning round to face the sea, he raised his hands and cried out in a voice filled with authority, "Wind, be still." Immediately, the winddied down. Once again, he raised his arms and called, "Waves, die down." Straight away, the surging of the waves ceased and the sea was like a millpond once more.

Jesus' disciples were utterly amazed by what they had just witnessed. They began muttering among themselves. One of them said, "Who is this? Even the wind and the waves obey him." (Mark 4 v 41)

"He must be God. Nobody else could have such authority over the wind and the waves."

"He is God. Praise him."

So Jesus' power and authority are finally being recognised on earth by the sons of men. And to further reinforce his claim to be God, Jesus performed another amazing miracle the minute he stepped ashore on the other side of the sea.

It was in the Gadarene area of Galilee that the fishing boat carrying Jesus and his disciples alighted. There, a ferocious, demon-filled man, his long, knotted hair streaming behind him and his wild arms waving in front of his twisted face, screeched out with terrifying force, "Jesus, Son of God, what do you want with us. Promise us you won't send us into the abyss."

Here the man flung himself at Jesus' feet. "Please, please," the distorted voice continued, "send us into that herd of pigs."

"What is your name?" asked Jesus, who was the only person there not cowering away from this demon-possessed creature.

"Legion. For we are many," threatened the voice.

Raising his eyes to heaven as he pointed at the demon-controlled man, he commanded, "Go into that herd of pigs." Immediately the man at Jesus' feet collapsed as though dead. At that very moment, the thousands of pigs that had been feeding quietly on the hill stampeded down towards the sea, launched themselves into the water, and one by one, they drowned themselves. But the man at Jesus' feet, who no longer had any demons living in him, quietly went off to clothe himself, then came back and asked the Master if he could come with him. Jesus, however, instructed him to go to his village and tell everyone how much God had done for him. The hard-hearted villagers, though, surprisingly asked Jesus to leave their region. In this case, the glory and power of God was not recognised on earth.

But we angels in heaven do recognise our Master's power and authority, therefore we will continue to praise and glorify him in any way we can.

Raphael
The Heavenly Chronicle

As soon as this wonderful news had been trumpeted across the heavens, the angels began to dance and sing. As if with one mind, they formed a semi-circle, then gracefully, like swans, they raised their necks, arms and wings, moving them up and down to the rhythm of the beating drums and clashing cymbals. As one by one, the different sections of the heavenly orchestra joined in – the violins, the clarinets, the flutes, the harps and the cellos – the angels lifted themselves up and waved their bodies from side to side. As the music reached its crescendo, in unison, the massed angels dipped down, mimicking the action of breaking waves. Their swaying, lifting and dipping movements were fast and furious as they imitated the drama of the storm.

And then, the angelic choir harmonised, "Be still", to the accompaniment of thousands of trumpets. Immediately, the angelic dance troupe became like statuettes, all freezing in their most recent position. They were at peace in their poses for quite a while until a dramatic drum roll announced a disturbance. An angel representing the demon-possessed man flung himself into the middle of the circle, writhing around. Angel voices, in beautiful harmony, rang out across the heavens, "Go into the herd of pigs."

The man's writhing body became still. He stood up and cried, "To God be the glory, great things he has done."

"Hallelujah, hallelujah. All praise and honour and glory and power belong to the King of Kings and Lord of Lords."

Although Raphael didn't witness this celebratory dance, he heard about it later from Gabriel and it made his heart sing. How glorious that he had been asked to contribute in a very small way to building a kingdom of praise to their great God, the father of all mankind, the creator and sustainer of the universe.

Chapter Fifteen

There didn't seem to be any rest for the Son of Man while he was on earth. He was constantly at work, healing more and more sick people and preaching the word of God to the multitudes. Raphael was being continually impressed by Jesus' boundless energy, his great compassion and his timeless words of wisdom. While it was great to see the crowds following him everywhere, sometimes Raphael doubted their sincerity. They were all for witnessing yet another wonder from this miracle worker of the moment, yet when he started to teach them important lessons, most of them, not least of whom were the Pharisees, the supposed teachers of the law, did not appear to have understood a word of what the Master had been saying to them.

Straight after Jesus had exercised his power in such a memorable way at the Gadarenes, he travelled by boat with his disciples to Capernaum. Here, as usual, he found himself to be much in demand, chiefly for his healing ministry. On one occasion, people kept streaming through the door of the house where many had gathered to hear him preach. Raphael saw that there were so many people crammed into the room where

Jesus was speaking that they were crushed against the walls; even the pathway outside the house was packed with men and women who were pushing to get in, so eager were they to hear from this new wonder-prophet and to see him executing the acts of a magician.

But amongst all those insincere hypocrites, Raphael had detected some genuine seekers for the truth; those who, when they saw Jesus, recognized in him someone who had the power not only to heal them, but also to save them. These were the people who listened intently to every word that Jesus said, following him around wherever he went.

Just then, Raphael was stirred from his reflections by a commotion at the door. Quickly, he went to see what was happening. There, lying on his mat, was a helpless, paralysed man. His friends were trying to elbow their way through the crowd. But some large men were blocking the door.

"Let us through, let us through," cried one of the men, his voice rising in desperation. "Our friend is very sick. He can't move at all. He has been suffering from paralysis for a very long time."

"Ha, you'll never get in there," scoffed the man who was standing closest to the door. "I've been trying since early morning, but I haven't moved forward an inch. There are far too many people in that room."

"It's positively unhealthy in there," said another man who was trying to get out. "Suffocating. You can't breathe in there. Better to stay outside."

"But we just have to get our friend to Jesus. We know he can heal him."

"Wait for him outside then."

"How long do you think he'll be in there?"

The man shrugged. "Anybody's guess. He's been known to stick around in the same house for days."

"Without coming out?"

"Without stepping foot out of the house."

The man turned away, defeated. He, with the help of his friends, carried the mat with the sick man on it a little further away.

"We've got to make a plan," said his friend.

"We'll never get in there. Too many people."

"What about the roof?" said another.

"That won't help."

"Yes it will. All we have to do is make a hole in the roof. Then we can lower our sick friend through it."

"You're not serious!"

"Come, help me... I'll climb up first with Joseph, then you two pass up our sick friend and his mat. You can all help taking up the tiles."

"You sure we should be doing this?"

"Of course. How else are we going to get our friend to Jesus?"

So Raphael watched in amazement as the four men methodically carried out their plan. He was particularly interested in the crowd's reaction as the man on the mat descended on them from above, landing directly in front of Jesus in a space that had just been vacated by a large man, who, fearing injury when he saw what was happening, just managed to get out of the way in the nick of time. Jesus stopped talking in mid-sentence and looked with great compassion at the paralysed man before him.

"Friend," he announced, "your sins are forgiven." (Luke 5 v 20)

That remark caused quite a stir. The Pharisees began to grumble about Jesus.

"Who are you to forgive sins!" one of them challenged.

"Yes. Only God can forgive sins," said another. "This is blasphemy."

Jesus looked at them directly and said, "Which is easier, to forgive sins or to heal this paralysed man? But that you may know that the Son of Man has authority on earth to forgive sins, I mantel you, get up, take your mat and go home." (Luke 5 v 24)

As Raphael had come to expect, the young man did indeed get up, pick up his mat and walk. "Praise be to God, praise be to God," he cried excitedly. Despite the crush, the people pushed back, making a path for him. "Praise be to God, praise be to God," he repeated. And then he began to dance.

Some of the people nearby started to clap. But the Pharisees continued to grumble among themselves about Jesus' claim to have authority for forgiving sins. Calmly, Jesus got up and followed the rejoicing man out into the street. There, he saw a notorious tax collector named Matthew sitting at a tax collector's booth. To everyone's great surprise, he approached the man and said in a loud, clear voice, "Follow me." Even more surprising was the man's response. Immediately, this tax collector who had a reputation for being duplicitous left his booth and followed Jesus.

But it didn't stop there. Jesus actually told Matthew that he needed to dine with him. He did what the Pharisees considered to be the ultimate taboo: to eat with a tax collector and other sinners. The group of Pharisees who were watching Jesus' actions had plenty to say about that. In fact, they now had even more ammunition to criticise Jesus.

"He dines with the worst of sinners," complained one Pharisee.

"If this were a godly man, he wouldn't dream of dining at a tax collector's house. Doesn't he know how these vermin cheat our people?" said another.

"I don't know how he can pollute himself by stooping so low. He is constantly making himself unclean."

But Jesus, knowing their thoughts and hearing their grumblings, turned to this group of self-righteous Pharisees and said, "It is not the healthy who need a doctor, but the sick. But go and learn what this means: 'I desire mercy, not sacrifice.' For I have not come to call the righteous, but sinners." (Matthew 9 vs 12-13)

Despite these words of wisdom and his reference to the book of Hosea, the Pharisees continued to grumble about Jesus, criticising him for not following the traditions of their nation and – the ultimate irony – for not ensuring that he remained pure. Why were they so blind? Couldn't they see for themselves how spotless Jesus was; that, though tempted like any other man, he never, ever committed even one sin in thought or in deed. Whereas the Pharisees... Raphael shuddered to think how hypocritical they were.

He knew, though, that the angelic host would have plenty to celebrate the minute they heard about what Jesus was continuing to do on the earth. So, as usual, he disciplined himself to pen yet another article that would be blared across the heavens from the trumpets and into the clouds, whipping up white wisps of cloud script until every celestial being would know how the Son of Man was continuing to glorify God through his behaviour and his actions.

Jesus heals a paralytic man and calls sinners to follow him

When Jesus came with his disciples to Capernaum, as usual, a large crowd awaited him. But wanting to preach the good news of the kingdom, he went inside a house to teach. Both men and women packed themselves into the house to listen to his words. So large was the crowd inside that it was impossible for anybody else to enter. Even the path leading to the front door was jammed with people who were unsuccessfully trying to push themselves in.

Four men approached, carrying a man who was lying very still at the centre of his mat. For it was quite clear that this man could not move: he was completely paralysed. They realised that they could not get into the house where they had heard that Jesus was teaching. But their sick, paralysed friend desperately needed Jesus' help.

So determined were these men to get their sick friend to Jesus, and so great was their faith, that they climbed up onto the roof, manoeuvred the man and his mat up to where they were and began to remove the roof tiles. When they had made a big enough hole, they proceeded to lower their friend. They managed to position him in such a way that he landed directly in front of Jesus. Everyone in that room was completely aghast except for Jesus, who looked with great compassion at the man and said, "Son, your sins are forgiven." (Mark 2 v 5)

At this, a man standing nearby, obviously a Pharisee judging by his attire, began to grumble aloud: "This man is blasphemous. Who can forgive sins but God alone."

Jesus turned to him and said, "Which is easier, to say to the paralytic, 'Your sins are forgiven,' or to say, 'Getup, take your mat and walk'? But that you may know that the Son of Man has authority on earth to forgive sins..." He said to the paralytic, "I tell you, get up, take your mat and go home." (Mark 2 vs 9-11)

To everyone's amazement, the paralysed man was instantly healed. As he walked with his mat, he immediately began to shout and sing praises to God. But the Pharisees continued to grumble: "It is the Sabbath. The law forbids a man to carry his mat on the Sabbath.

Indeed, it is forbidden to do any work whatsoever on the Sabbath, the sacred day of the Lord. How dare this man heal on the Sabbath."

But they had more to grumble about. When Jesus had finished teaching in that house, he went outside and saw a tax collector named Matthew sitting at his booth. Without hesitation, he said, "Follow me." Immediately, Matthew got up from his booth and followed Jesus. To add insult to injury, as far as the Pharisees were concerned, he invited himself in to dine with the man.

"How can he dine with sinners? If that man were a prophet, he would not go into the house of a sinful tax collector! And he certainly would not go in to dine with him. Our law forbids us to do unclean things, and eating with a wicked tax collector makes a man filthily unclean. Polluted. No, this man is not a prophet, otherwise he would keep our law."

Once again, Jesus turned to the Pharisee who had been saying these things and said, "It is not the healthy who need a doctor, but the sick. I have not come to call the righteous, but sinners." Mark 2 v 17)

Once again, Jesus has displayed his authority on earth to forgive sins, perform astounding miracles and to call sinners to himself. It is right and meet to praise him, the mighty and gracious Son of God himself as he ministers to all God's people on earth.

Raphael
The Heavenly Chronicle

As usual, the message was sent swiftly into the heavens on the wings of the air and the trumpet blasts. And as usual, the angels assembled with joy in their hearts and praise in their voices as this time, they sang a dance drama to their Lord and their King. The drama was dramatic, powerful and uplifting. It began with the waiting crowds. They were singing a song as they looked expectantly into the dusty road. The angels pretending to be citizens of the world flung their arms into the air; some of them stamped their feet; others sashayed to the left and the right. Their song was repetitive, but its volume increased as the expectancy of the waiting crowd grew to fever pitch:

"We are waiting, waiting, waiting, waiting,

Waiting for a miracle – a miracle;

We are waiting, waiting, waiting, waiting…

Waiting for a miracle – a wonderful miracle.

Who has the power to perform a miracle?

Who can show us an impossible feat?

Who is the miracle worker from Nazareth.

Jesus, the Son of Joseph."

As the angel representing Jesus actually approached the crowd, his approach prompted the drummers, cymbal players, tambourine shakers and trumpeters to announce his arrival with loud pomp and tuneful ceremony.

A group representing his disciples sang a different kind of song:

"He has come to teach us…

We have come to learn;

He teaches us in parables…

We try to understand…

He interprets the Scriptures…

We listen to him;

He shows us the way of God…

We open our eyes."

At that moment, there was a loud commotion above them represented by a banging and clashing of the drums and cymbals. The narrator looked up in alarm. "But what is that noise? It is coming from the roof? Who is trying to disturb our peace? Who is trying to spoil our teaching? Look! A man is being lowered from the roof! Look! The man cannot walk. He is lying on a mat. And his friends are looking on. Look! He has landed at Jesus' feet. What will Jesus do? Will he perform a miracle? Is this the miracle that we have all been waiting for? Will we see yet another amazing miracle from Jesus, Son of Joseph from Nazareth? Watch carefully. See what this miracle worker can do. See what feat he can perform. But the people do not get what they expect – not at first. And the Pharisees certainly don't get what they have anticipated. They were all watching the man's legs, but instead, Jesus spoke to his heart."

The rich voice of a solo tenor filled the heavens with Jesus' words: "Son, your sins are forgiven."

The sick man bowed his head in humility and with thanks. Jesus touched the man's head, looking at him with great compassion.

The base voice of a shocked Pharisee sang: "This is not allowed. This is not permitted. This is blasphemy. Blasphemy." At this, he tore at his robe. "Blasphemy. Blasphemy," intoned his deep bass. "This will not be tolerated by our nation. For who can forgive sins but God alone."

A group of 'Pharisees' echoed the bass singer's sentiments: "God alone can forgive sins. Who is this man to play God? No man can forgive sins. That privilege belongs to God alone."

"But Jesus is standing up," continued the narrator. "Jesus is facing his accusers. Jesus is looking them directly in the eye. Jesus is saying: (Here the choir loudly chanted Jesus' words, making them powerfully alive) 'Which is easier: to forgive a man's sins or to heal him? But so that you may know that the Son of God has authority on earth to forgive sins, (here, he turned to the paralysed man) I say to you, young man, get up, take your mat and walk.'"

"Look," boomed the narrator. "The miracle the crowd has been waiting for. The amazing act that the Pharisees had been expecting. The marvellous event that they were waiting to criticise. Because this was the Sabbath. How dare Jesus heal on the Sabbath?

"This man is walking. How can that be? He is carrying his mat. This is impossible! This man is healed. He is singing. He is dancing. He is praising the Lord. But the Pharisees are grumbling, they are criticising, they are plotting against Jesus. And as if this were not enough, Jesus goes outside and invites himself in to a tax collector's house. How dare he pollute himself by dining with a sinner! If he were a prophet, he wouldn't dream of dining at a tax collector's house and making himself unclean. But Jesus is unperturbed. He knows how to speak the words of God. He doesn't need man's testimony because he knows what is in the heart of a man."

The rich tenor sang out Jesus' words with much conviction:

"It is the not the healthy I have come to call; it is the sick.

Healthy people do not need a doctor; the sick need a doctor.

I have come to heal the sick; I have come to make them well again.

I have not come for the righteous, but for sinners."

The loud, angry voices of the Pharisees were now represented with a crescendo of the drums and a clanging of the cymbals. But then the sweet, pure voice of the harp trilled out a melody of forgiveness and love which was so powerful that all of the assembled angels were deeply moved and began, once again, to praise God for his love, his grace and his forgiveness.

It was at times like this that Raphael wished he could be right in the midst of the heavenly throng. He missed the corporate worship, most of all the choirs of angels lifting their voices in unison to praise the God of the universe and his only son, Jesus, who was carrying out his mission on the earth. Sometimes, he longed to be in the heavenly realms again amongst all that joy and contentment. What a privilege it was, and how fulfilling, to be celebrating the Lord's wonderful deeds and Jesus' power and authority with all the other angels, and carrying out their mission of praise throughout the whole heavens.

However, he was deeply aware of his new responsibility, and that right now, his mission was very different from what it had been in heaven. For just a moment, he chided himself for not being joyful about his new mission. He had been sent to perform a special task, and he should be putting his whole heart and soul into doing it to the best of his ability. He found himself reflecting on his Lord and Master's humility. That Jesus, the Son of God himself, should humble himself to such an extent that he had come to live among sinful man, was almost too astounding to be true. Yet there, below him on the earth, was the daily evidence of this truth: Jesus walking with men and women, talking with them, teaching them, eating with them, healing them, drawing children to himself – when he could, instead, be in the heavenly realms communing with his Father right now.

But he was patiently talking to Peter, that impulsive son of men who often made mistakes because of his brashness. He looked very flustered, and had just come directly to Jesus after an aggressive, finger-pointing Pharisee had been questioning him. Raphael drew closer so that he could overhear what his Master wanted to teach Peter.

"Master, Master," he said, "the collectors of the two drachma tax have been harassing me. That Pharisee over there has just asked me if my teacher pays the temple tax. I didn't know what to say to him."

"Peter, Peter," replied Jesus, compassion filling his eyes. "From whom do the kings of the earth collect duty and taxes - from their own sons or from others?"(Matthew 17 v 25)

Immediately, Peter replied, "From others."

"Then the sons are exempt,"(Matthew 17 v 26) replied Jesus. He paused, but Peter only looked half relieved. He glanced over his shoulder at the scornful Pharisee who had accosted him.

Jesus gazed at him understandingly and continued: "But so that we don't offend them, go, throw out your line. Take the first fish you catch; open its mouth and you will find a four drachma coin. Take it and give it to them for my tax and yours." (Matthew 17 v 27)

Now Peter looked genuinely relieved. With no hesitation, he carried out to the letter his Master's instructions. Sure enough, when Peter opened the mouth of the first fish he caught, he found that four drachma coin. Hurriedly, he took it to the tax collector. But instead of looking pleased, the on-looking Pharisee's mouth twisted with displeasure. It did cross Raphael's mind that nothing seemed to please those seemingly permanently discontented and joy-squashing Pharisees. He decided that even this humble incident-miracle was worth recording and celebrating in the heavenly realms because it demonstrated Jesus' total power and authority over all worldly concerns.

This time, Raphael took particular pleasure in writing his article and passing up the news of Jesus' total control of worldly affairs.

Jesus' miraculous coin foils the Pharisee

On a busy afternoon in Capernaum, Jesus once again foiled the 'authority' of the sons of men: he miraculously produced two coins so that Peter could pay his own and his Master's tax. Once again, the Son of God demonstrated his power and his genuine authority over all things.

With the obvious intention of discrediting Jesus, a Pharisee had scornfully asked Peter whether his teacher paid the two drachma temple tax. Flustered, Jesus' disciple approached his Master and told him what the Pharisee had said. As so often happens with the Master, he calmly turned the whole situation around by asking his follower a question: "Do the Kings of the earth collect taxes from their own sons or from others?" he said.

"From others," replied Peter, still looking rather flustered.

"Well then, the sons are exempt," said Jesus, pausing to see Peter's reaction. Peter only looked half relieved as he glanced over his shoulder at the Pharisee, who by now appeared to be triumphantly scornful. But again, as so often happens when Jesus is present amongst his followers, he trumped that Pharisee. Looking directly into Peter's eyes, Jesus said to him, "But so that we do not offend them, go, throw out your line: open the mouth of the first fish you catch. Inside his mouth, you will find a four drachma coin. Take that coin and give it to them for my tax and yours."

Immediately, Peter followed his Master's instructions. He threw out his line and caught a fish straight away.

Hurriedly, he opened the mouth of the fish. A big smile broke across his face when he pulled that four drachma coin from the fish's mouth. When Peter went to pay the tax, however, the Pharisee was not pleased. He had been trumped! And he didn't like it. He darted a savage look at Peter and his Master. So Jesus is making enemies amongst the sons of men who obstinately refuse to recognise who he is and what he has come to earth to do. If only they could open their eyes so that they, too, could be saved!

Raphael
The Heavenly Chronicle

As soon as he had completed his article, Raphael thought he heard a double 'Hallelujah' coursing through the airwaves towards him. What he didn't know was right at that moment in heaven, the angels were composing a new song about Christ the Redeemer's activities among the sons of men. He only heard that song much, much later when his earthly ministry was over. In the meanwhile, he continued to be dumbfounded about how little the sons of men understood about this 'man', Jesus, who was walking amongst them, teaching them and encouraging them to come to him. If only more of them would genuinely put their trust in him and follow where he led. But seemingly, each man, woman and child was called to make his own decision about who this Jesus was. And apparently, how few of them accepted this great blessing: all they had to do was to turn to Jesus and be saved! How hard could that be! Especially as he was the perfect 'Son of Man' with not even a trace of sin. Why couldn't they see that he was unique? Raphael was amazed by their blindness and prayed that the scales would fall from their eyes.

Chapter Sixteen

Raphael marvelled at all the good news stories he kept having the privilege of reporting. He also marvelled at the reactions of different groups of people to these wonderfully amazing stories of healing and forgiveness. While a small group of Jesus' followers were clearly genuinely moved and affected by these miracles – to the extent that they put their faith in Jesus – the majority were just waiting for the next sensational event so that they could tell their friends, and spread the news about the extraordinary wonder-worker from Nazareth – of all places. For as everybody knew, nothing good had ever come from Nazareth.

It was when Jesus and his disciples were on their way to Jerusalem, travelling along the border between Samaria and Galilee, that Raphael witnessed yet another extraordinary miracle, but also found himself being disappointed at the reaction of most sons of men to the Son of God's power and compassion.

As Jesus approached a village, ten men with leprosy met him on the road. However, used to being spurned by everybody, they did stand at a distance from him, calling out in loud voices, "Jesus, Master, have pity on us."

Jesus turned around, looked at them with compassion and said, "Go, show yourselves to the priests." Obediently, although some of them had confused expressions, they went on their way. As they were walking, they were cleansed – completely healed of their serious affliction.

One of them, when he saw he was healed, came back, praising God in a loud voice. He – a Samaritan – threw himself at Jesus' feet and thanked him profusely. Raphael found himself empathising with his Master's next words: "Were not all ten cleansed? Where are the other nine? Was no-one found to return and give praise to God except this foreigner?" (Luke 17 vs 17-18) How ungrateful were most men! How they took the Son of God's extraordinary miracles for granted! Why were their hearts so hard and selfish!

But Jesus, full of compassion for the one man who had come back with a thankful heart, praising God, said to him: "Rise and go; your faith has made you well." (Luke 17 v 19)

But for Raphael, the greatest surprise had come from the most unexpected source. The 'learned' men, those who not only studied the Scriptures all day long but also devised rule after rule for pure living, were the ones who more than opposed Jesus: they considered him their enemy; they hated him so much that they wanted to kill him. And what was their motive? None other than the dangerous sin of envy – jealousy – the deadly sins they had been warned about by many prophets. And if they didn't watch themselves, the deadly sins would be their downfall, even unto death.

Despite the regular opposition of the Pharisees – they frequently asked him questions with the sole intention of trapping him in his words, and on a number of heart-stopping occasions, picked up stones, ironically, to stone Jesus, the Son of God, for blasphemy – Jesus continued unabatedly with his ministry of teaching and healing. In every situation that unfolded in front of Raphael's eyes, Jesus' compassion was evident.

So one day, when a young ruler threw himself at the Master's feet, straight away, Jesus reached out his hand to touch the man. With a voice full of emotion, the young ruler said: "Master, my young daughter has just died. She is only twelve years old and she is the pride of my life. But even now, although she has died, I know that you can bring her back to life." Jesus looked directly at him and in a calm, steady voice, said, "I will go with you."

So, sensing something important was about to happen, the crowd followed Jesus, his disciples and this young ruler. From a distance, Raphael could hear the loud wailing and the mournful, funereal sounds of the lutes. The dancers who were hired to mark tragic situations like this one were also in attendance.

As Jesus approached the house, he said to the young ruler, in a loud voice so everyone could hear, "The child is not dead but asleep." (Mark 5 v 39)

At this, there was an outcry. Some standing nearby said, "How can he be so insensitive?"

"Yes, he is making the family's suffering worse. This child has been dead for some time."

"He shouldn't be allowed to give false hope."

"It's not right."

"Where are you going, Sir?" asked one of the family.

"To wake up the sleeping girl."

"Sir, this girl really is dead. I touched her lifeless body myself. She has no pulse. She has no breath. All my relatives can testify to that. That is why we have brought in the mourners. If she were alive, there would be no need for funereal wailing and dancing."

"Let me through with the parents of the child, and with these two disciples."

Raphael saw the man shaking his head vigorously, but the man did stand aside to let Jesus, the parents and the disciples through. The angel expected Jesus to do something dramatic – like laying himself fully across the body of the girl, as Elijah had done – but he simply looked up to heaven, then said in a loud, clear voice: "Little girl, I say to you, get up." (Mark 5, v 41)

The young girl stirred. She rubbed her eyes, sat up slowly and stretched her arms. She did, indeed, look as if she had just been in a deep, deep sleep. The people in that room had little time to respond in amazement. For Jesus was completely practical. "Give her something to eat," he said simply, then quietly vacated the room.

Then next thing Raphael saw as Jesus and his disciples unobtrusively slipped away from that place was the shock, awe, surprise and excitement of all the onlookers as that young girl walked out of that room – alive.

Hardly had the disciples had time to digest this extraordinary miracle, arguably the most impossible that Jesus had yet done, than another mind-shattering event happened not far from that young ruler's home. Typically, the throngs were pressing around Jesus as he walked along the dusty road. But all of a sudden, he stopped abruptly and cried out, "Who touched me?" (Mark 5 v 31))Raphael had seen what had happened. So he understood why Peter had said to his Master, "But there are people pressing in on you from every side. Scores of people must be touching you right now." From his elevated position, Raphael had seen something that Peter had not. He had seen a thin, dark woman in a long robe which was stained with a dark smear of blood at the back, inching closer and closer to Jesus. This woman had approached him from the back, her veiled head downcast. Those nearest to her, when they saw the dark stain of blood, had pushed away from her, ironically making a path for her. Quick as a flash, she had taken her opportunity. She had reached out her hand and placed the tips of her fingers gently on the edge of Jesus' robe. Once again, to Peter's great surprise, Jesus said, "Who touched me?" There was silence. But Raphael could see the woman trembling.

"Someone touched me? I know that power has gone out from me." (Luke 8 v 46)

"Sir… " came the tremulous voice from behind him. Jesus turned and looked down with great love at the woman kneeling at his feet.

"Yes, my daughter," Jesus said softly.

Raphael witnessed the floodgates opening. This poor woman who had been in extreme suffering poured out her heart to Jesus: "Sir, I have been suffering for twelve long years with what I thought was an incurable illness. I have been bleeding – without stopping – for twelve very long years. The physical suffering was severe, the pain was sometimes agonising, but I could have endured that. What was worse – much, much worse – was being scorned and rejected by my family, my friends, and even the synagogue rulers and the priests. I have been unclean for these twelve long years, surviving by snatching what I could from leftovers that people would find it hard to give to their pigs. But now you have made me well again. My bleeding has stopped. Quite suddenly. The minute I touched your robe. I knew you could make me better."

"Daughter, your faith has healed you. Go in peace and be freed from your suffering." (Mark 5 v 34)

What stories to announce to the angelic hosts. What a privilege to be given such an important task. How he loved to glorify the Father through the Son in this way. Raphael wasted no time in getting to work.

Jesus raises a young girl from the dead and heals a broken woman

As Jesus was walking along the road with a large crowd of his disciples, a young ruler from the region approached him and said, "My twelve-year-old daughter has just died, but even now, you can raise her to life."

Willing as ever to continue with his healing ministry, Jesus said, "I will go with you." But as he approached the man's house, the loud wailing, the mournful sounds of the lute players and the sombre dancing of the funereal mourners could be seen and heard.

"Your daughter is not dead; she is sleeping," Jesus said to the gathering of family, friends and mourners. But every single person there testified that the ruler's daughter was indeed dead.

Jesus merely repeated, "The girl is not dead; she is sleeping." So, taking the girl's parents and two of his closest disciples into the room where the young girl lay, after looking up to heaven, he commanded, "Little(Mark 5 v 41) girl, I say to you, get up."

After the girl had rubbed her eyes, stretched and sat up, looking around bewildered, as if she had been woken from a deep, deep sleep, Jesus instructed them to give her something to eat.

Before the disciples could even digest the enormity of this miracle, a crowd was pressing in on him from all around. He stopped, abruptly, in the middle of the road.

"Who touched me?" (Luke 8 v 45) he cried. The disciples pointed out that there were many people touching him at that very moment, as the crowds were pressing in on him from every side. But Jesus insisted that the power had gone out of him.

At this, a woman, realising she could not slip away unnoticed, admitted that she had touched Jesus deliberately. She testified that she had been suffering from bleeding for twelve long years, and that she had spent everything she had on doctors, to no avail, for no-one had managed to cure her. But the minute she touched the hem of Jesus' garment, she was instantly healed. Our always compassionate Master said to her, "Daughter, your faith has healed you. Go in peace. " (Luke 8 v 48)

So yet again, the Son of God's great compassion, grace and love has been demonstrated to the sons of men.

Raphael
The Heavenly Chronicle

This time, the heavens were ablaze with light. From one end of the sky to the other, every heavenly light in the cosmos, all the suns, stars and planets, seemed to be streaming across the universe. So bright and so glorious was this heavenly celebration that Raphael, all the way back on earth, had to shield his eyes from its brilliance. Jesus, the creator and sustainer of the universe, was, by his father's will, the incomparable Christ, the Messiah, the Saviour of the World. No wonder the heavens were intent on displaying his glory.

Chapter Seventeen

Although a very long time before Jesus' mission on earth, Raphael had witnessed Jesus' glory in heaven, he continued to be in awe of the Son of God's power and authority. He was witnessing so many miracles now that he couldn't possibly record and relay all of them. He was conscious of the responsibility he had to reveal how prophecy was being fulfilled: "Then will the eyes of the blind be opened and the ears of the deaf unstopped. Then will the lame leap like a deer, and the mute tongue shout for joy." (Isaiah 35 vs 5–6) What he also continued to be amazed by was man's reaction to all these miracles. While some men and women were grateful, praising God for all the extraordinary marvels they were witnessing, the majority appeared to be unmoved, whilst some, particularly those in authority like the Pharisees, were blatantly antagonistic.

How anybody could criticise Jesus for restoring men, women and children and making them whole was completely beyond Raphael's understanding. Of course, when they wanted something, the people recognised their need for Jesus. He was, after all, the latest wonder-man – a miracle worker who could perform deeds that were considered to be impossible for everybody else. If only the people would open their eyes to see the significance of what was happening in front of their very eyes.

As miracles were expected of Jesus, the sick, the blind, the lame and the families of the demon-possessed followed him through the dusty streets, into homes, onto the mountainside, by the river and next to the lake.

Raphael continued to marvel at the Master's patience as huge crowds constantly followed him, pressing up against him. One morning when Jesus had left Tyre and was near Sidon, he went down to the Sea of Galilee in the region of the Decapolis. Raphael saw a group of men urgently marching towards Jesus with an afflicted man. Their spokesman said to Jesus, "Teacher, this man is deaf and can barely talk. Please will you place your hand on him and heal him."

As usual, Jesus looked with compassion on the afflicted man. Raphael witnessed the Master drawing him aside so that he was away from the crowd. Looking directly at the man, Jesus put his fingers in his ears. He then spat so that his saliva landed on his tongue. He looked up to heaven and with a sigh, said, "Eph-Phatha!" (Be opened.) (Mark 7 v 34)

As soon as Jesus had said this, astonishingly, the man began to speak in a way that everyone could understand. His companions were amazed.

Jesus said quietly to this man he had healed, "Don't tell anyone what has happened to you."

But the man was so excited that he couldn't stop talking about what Jesus had done for him. Raphael realised, judging by the increased numbers of people who insisted on seeing

Jesus, that this news was making it very difficult for Jesus to teach his disciples. The crowds were amazed and the man was overwhelmed. The people began saying of Jesus: "He has done everything well. He even makes the deaf hear and the mute speak." (Mark 7 v 37)

Raphael, rejoicing in his heart, was just about to record this incident when he witnessed more desperate men calling for Jesus.

In the heat of the day, two blind men, groping desperately for Jesus, were calling out in loud voices as they heard him going by. "Have mercy on us, Son of David." (Matthew 9 v 27) Jesus, who was on the point of going indoors, turned to them and asked, "Do you believe I am able to do this?" They both replied at once, "Yes Lord." Jesus leant towards them and touched their eyes, saying in a tone of authority mixed with compassion, "According to your faith will it be done to you." (Matthew 9 v 29) Immediately, both men threw up their arms, twirled around and shouted, "We can see. We can see." Jesus, however, said to them, "See that nobody knows about this." But there was no stopping these men. They were so overjoyed that their sight had been restored that they rushed to tell their families, their acquaintances and even strangers about how they were blind, but now they could see.

The news about Jesus spread so quickly throughout that region that it became very difficult for him to teach the people about the kingdom of God.

Very soon after the miraculous healing of the blind men, some concerned family members brought a man who could not speak to Jesus. "It is very hard to live with this man," they said. "He is possessed by a wicked demon who prevents him from speaking. We cannot understand him at all. And what is worse, we're scared of our own relative! He flings himself around and strikes out at us. Please can you help us."

Jesus looked at the afflicted man and said, "Demon, come out of this man." At once, the man straightened up and began to speak in a normal voice. Many of the people standing around shouted out in amazement. One of the men near Jesus said, "Nothing like this has ever been seen in Israel." (Matthew 9 v 33) But amongst the crowd, there were also members of the ruling sect. A group of Pharisees, their robes flowing and their long phylacteries on display to impress the people, were huddled together, pointing at Jesus and debating amongst themselves. One of them, the one with the longest phylactery of all, approached Jesus, standing directly in front of him. But he did not look at him. Instead, he deliberately turned away from Jesus and faced the crowd. Gesturing towards Jesus with his right arm, but not even deigning to engage in any eye contact, he said in a loud, important-sounding, dogmatic voice, "It is by the prince of demons that he drives out demons." (Matthew 9 v 34)The crowd gasped. Some of them even recoiled from Jesus.

But the Master remained completely calm, saying in a voice of authority: "How can Satan drive out Satan? If a kingdom is divided against itself, that kingdom cannot stand… No one can enter a strong man's house and carry off his possessions unless he first ties up the strong man." (Mark 3 vs 24- 27) Then he said something that should have shocked the Pharisees rigid. But they seemed to be totally unfazed by his stern warning: "all the sins and blasphemies of men will be forgiven them. But whoever blasphemes against the Holy

Spirit will never be forgiven; he is guilty of an eternal sin." (Mark 3 vs 28-29)

Furious that Jesus had said this in the presence of the people, and anxious about the impression his words would create on the crowd, they clustered around each other again and began to plot Jesus' downfall. Who did these men think they were to go against the living God? Who were they to oppose the Son of God himself? Had they even considered what would happen to them on judgement day? Or did they believe that they were totally above the law! Raphael knew that he had to allow events to unfold below him on the earth. It wasn't his place to interfere in the plan of the Lord Almighty. But he felt so incensed by these hypocrites that he wanted to do something to glorify God. The only thing he could think of doing right now was to write his article in which he could celebrate Christ's power and authority over men on this earth. He felt much better once he had begun to pen his article, which, as usual, was trumpeted across the heavens the minute his words hit the scrolled clouds.

Jesus heals two blind men and casts out a demon

A large crowd was following Jesus. He was about to enter a house when he was approached by two blind men who cried out in loud voices, "Son of David. Have mercy on us."

Jesus, when he saw the condition of these two men, said to them, "Do you believe I am able to do this?" (Matthew 9 v 28)

They both replied, "Yes, Sir."

So he said to them, "According to your faith,

will it be done to you." (Matthew 9 v 29)

Immediately, the two men began to jump for joy, clap and sing out aloud, "We can see."

When their elation had subsided a little, Jesus said to them, "See that no-one knows about this." (Matthew 9 v 30)

But the two men went and told their relatives and their friends. Now even more people follow Jesus everywhere, some of them praising God and listening intently to his teaching. The Son of Man continues to make an impact on the earth amongst the sons of men.

Scarcely had this amazing miracle been completed than a group of people rushed up to Jesus and told him about their mute relative. They said a demon had inhabited the man and they asked for Jesus' help. The Son of God didn't waste any time in commanding the demon to come out of him. When he began to speak in a normal voice and demonstrated that he was in his right mind, his relatives praised God.

Not so the Pharisees who were standing nearby. They muttered and grumbled among themselves, one of them saying, "It is by the prince of demons that he drives out demons." (Matthew 9 v 34) Calmly, Jesus proceeded to give them a lesson in logic. He explained that a house divided against itself could not stand. He gave a practical example of thieves having to tie up a strong man before they could rob him. Still, the Pharisees muttered and grumbled.

So Jesus gave them a stern warning: blasphemies against the Holy Spirit would not be forgiven and that sons of men who sinned in this way were in danger of the fires of hell. Once again, Jesus, the Son of God, has demonstrated his power and authority on earth to heal and to speak the truth, even in the face of opposition. All praise and honour and glory to our King of King and Lord of Lords.

Raphael
The Heavenly Chronicle

Apart from being so melodious, this time, the celestial celebration was so loud that Raphael didn't even have to move from his position to hear it. So he remained hovering above Jesus, in any case, not wanting to miss any events that Jesus might still perform on the earth. It was so exciting to watch the speed with which he helped people, his overarching compassion for all mankind, even the worst of the sinners, and the miraculous results he achieved by merely uttering words of command to demons and to every kind of disease known to man.

As Raphael waited in anticipation for the next remarkable event to occur, he thought about the privilege that had been granted to him to watch, listen and record the actions of Jesus Christ himself, his King of Kings and Lord of Lords.

Chapter Eighteen

It didn't surprise Raphael that the next miraculous event happened in the temple on the Sabbath. And sadly, what didn't surprise him either, after all the occasions before where he had observed the lawmakers in action, was how the Pharisees reacted.

As usual on the Sabbath day, there were crowds of people at the temple, the women in the outer courts and the men in the inner courts. There were also many stallholders selling doves, pigeons, sheep and other animals for sacrifice. Groups of men were listening to the teachers who were explaining the word of God to them. But Raphael was only interested in hovering near one teacher, Jesus, to see what he would do and say to display God's glory. The angel often wondered why he, a lowly angel, had been granted the privilege of observing the Son of God at close range as he went about performing God's work on earth.

Although on a number of occasions already, Raphael had seen some of the Pharisees not acting in accordance with God's will, on this particular Sabbath, he was shocked to hear what a group of Pharisees were talking about within the temple itself, and almost within earshot of Jesus.

"We must put a stop to all this miraculous nonsense," said one of them. "This man," he continued, pointing at Jesus, "is gaining far too many followers."

"I quite agree," nodded another Pharisee. "He even speaks against our traditions and unsettles the people. If he were a prophet, he would follow our customs and observe all our laws. Moses would never have disrespected our Sabbath the way this man does."

The first Pharisee looked thoughtful. He scanned the crowd of men clustering around Jesus and found what he was looking for: a reason to accuse the man! He said to his colleague: "Let us test him to see if he will break the Sabbath laws yet again. Look, that man's right hand is completely shrivelled."

A crafty smile spread across his fellow conspirator's face. Approaching the man with the afflicted hand, he stood nearby and cleared his throat. Jesus noticed the man with the deformed hand. Immediately, he turned to him, a compassionate expression on his face. But before he could say or do anything, the Pharisee said to him, "Tell us, teacher, is it lawful to heal on the Sabbath?" (Luke 14 v 3)

Raphael could tell that Jesus knew exactly what the Pharisee was thinking. He returned his gaze steadily and said in a loud voice so that all the people standing around could hear him: "Which is lawful on the Sabbath: to do good or to do evil; to save life or to kill?" (Mark 3 v 4)

Jesus' question was met with silence. Nobody was prepared to answer him. So he continued: "If any of you has a sheep and it falls into a pit on the Sabbath, will you not take hold of it and lift it out?" (Matthew 12 v 11)

Again there was silence.

Deliberately, Jesus turned to the man with the shrivelled hand and said: "Come and stand here in front of everyone."

Immediately, the man obeyed him.

"Stretch out your hand." (Mark 4 v 5)

As soon as he did so, he let out a shriek of delight. Raphael could see why. The man's right hand was completely restored. It was just as sound as the other one. "Look, I am well again," the man cried out. "My hand... it is normal. Completely normal."

Everyone nearby who examined the man's hand was amazed. "How extraordinary," said a neighbour.

"What an amazing miracle," said another.

But the Pharisees were furious.

They clustered together in a huddle and began to discuss this event amongst themselves. Raphael thought it prudent to listen to them for a while, so that he could see what they thought of Jesus' latest miracle.

"This man is undermining our authority," said one.

"He must be stopped," said another.

"How are we going to stop him?" said one of the Herodians standing within earshot. "He has such a following."

"I agree. The masses adore him!"

"We need to get one of his disciples on our side."

"Good idea. Someone who knows his movements. It's no good arresting this Jesus when all the crowds are following him. We need to get him on his own."

"Yes. Find out where he goes with his disciples – when he withdraws from the crowd."

"It shouldn't be that difficult to bribe one of his disciples. Everyone loves money. Maybe we can work on the guy in charge of the money bags."

"You mean Judas?"

"Yes. I think he will be amenable to a bribe. It's getting more and more urgent. We can't let the number of Jesus' followers increase even more. Already the Roman governors are getting annoyed with us."

"We must exert our authority over the mob."

"You realise we'll have to do something extreme."

"Like killing the man? But the Romans won't allow us to do that."

"How about an assassination attempt?"

"We'll never get away with that. The Romans will crucify us."

"Well then we'll have to get the Romans on our side."

"How are we going to do that?"

"That's easy. All we have to do is get them to believe that this Jesus is a threat to the state, and to their authority."

"Some of the people are already calling him the king of the Jews."

"Exactly. So it shouldn't be too difficult to get the Romans to believe that this Jesus is a threat to their authority and to the stability of the country."

"But the people love him!"

"Precisely. But the people are notoriously fickle. And we can easily produce false witnesses who will testify against Jesus."

"We'll have to act quickly. Look how the people are crowding around Jesus and hanging on his every word."

"It's ridiculous how influenced the common man is with miracles. A wonder-worker from nowhere – Nazareth of all places – arrives in town and the people follow him slavishly."

"If the people were more discerning, they would know that it's against the law to perform miracles on our sacred Sabbath."

"Indeed! There are six other days every week. Why can't this Jesus perform his miracles on any of those other days? If he were a genuine prophet from God, he would know the law. And he would make sure that he did no work on the Sabbath."

"Let's go and seek out this Judas. It's about time we had a chat to him."

"Perhaps he will come to us first. Let's wait and see. We don't want to be seen to be consorting with Jesus' disciples."

"It would be better if he came to us first, but we can't wait forever. And we must be careful that we don't do anything on the Sabbath, or near the Passover. We must uphold the law. And be an example to the people."

Raphael could listen no longer. He was disgusted by this hypocritical talk and desperate to send out one of his positive headlines from heaven. Thank goodness the news associated with Jesus was always good news and that the headlines he penned about the Son of God were so inspiring to all the angels in the heavenly realms, even if Jesus' actions weren't appreciated by the sinful and hypocritical sons of men.

With great determination, Raphael took hold of his stylus and, with joy in his heart, he composed yet another good news article so that the angels of God could celebrate the awesome actions of the Son of God on earth.

Jesus' sensational healing of a man with a shrivelled hand

On the Sabbath day in Jerusalem, Jesus was teaching in the temple. As usual, there were crowds and crowds of people listening to him, but there were also the afflicted trying to get near him so that they could be healed.

The Pharisees, who knew of Jesus' reputation, wanted to test him: they wanted to see whether he would break their own man-made restrictive law which prevented anybody from healing a man on the Sabbath. They were deliberately looking for a reason to accuse Jesus, and it didn't take them long to find one.

A man with a shrivelled right hand gave them a perfect opportunity to accuse Jesus. So they approached the Master and said, "Teacher, tell us, is it lawful to heal on the Sabbath?"

Jesus indicated by his expression that he knew their thoughts, especially as they were pointing to the man with the shrivelled right hand who was by now very close to Jesus. The wonderful Son of God remained calm, saying to the Pharisees, "Which is lawful on the Sabbath: to do good or to do evil; to save life or to kill?" (Mark 3 v 4) When nobody answered him, he continued, "If any of you has a sheep and it falls into a pit on the Sabbath, will you not take hold of it and lift it out? How much more valuable is a man than a sheep!" (Matthew 12 vs 11-12) Nobody had anything to say in response, so the Master said to the man with the shrivelled hand, "Come and stand here in front of everyone." The man immediately obeyed. Jesus said, "Stretch out your hand." (Matthew 12 v 13

When the man did so, everyone, including the Pharisees, could see that the man's hand was completely restored. There was much rejoicing amongst the people, but instead of being happy that the afflicted man was now well again, the Pharisees went out and plotted how they might kill Jesus.

The Son of God continues to meet with serious opposition amongst the sons of men, particularly those in authority like the religious leaders, but again and again, the ordinary people are amazed at the extraordinary miracles they are witnessing; many of them are praising God for the miraculous healings and assume that Jesus is a prophet from God. If only more of the sons of men could open their eyes to see who Jesus really is; the Son of God himself.

Raphael
The Heavenly Chronicle

The choirs of angels didn't waste any time in praising Jesus and his Father. Their songs and instruments sounded particularly urgent to Raphael that day. The music was so loud that it sounded to Raphael as if they were trying to make up for the deficiencies in the sons of men. If the people on earth couldn't give the Son of God the praise, honour and glory due to him, the angels in heaven could certainly do their best to show God and his beloved Son just how much they owed him. In fact, that all the praises they could give in the heavenly realms would never be enough to show the King of Kings and

Lord of Lords just how much they appreciated his glorious majesty and perfect justice.

But hot on the heels of this miracle, Jesus performed two more, both of them on the Sabbath, which opened him up to more criticism from the Pharisees.

In the first, he showed compassion to a crippled woman; in the second, he healed a man of the debilitating disease, dropsy.

It always gladdened Raphael's heart to see Jesus teaching in one of the synagogues. Even though the Pharisees were so critical of him, they never managed to refute anything he taught – and this was not from a lack of trying. They were constantly laying verbal traps for him, hoping to catch him out so he could be discredited in the eyes of the people. The people, however, seemed to delight in his teaching as they clustered around him, avidly listening to him and marvelling at his words.

But even in the synagogue, people, including women, often desperately approached him to be healed of their afflictions. One day, as Raphael was listening to his Master's awe-inspiring words, he noticed a woman who was completely bent over. When questioned by a bystander, her companion replied, "She's been like this for eighteen long years, and she cannot straighten up at all. She experiences severe back and neck pain, and she has to be helped to perform most of her daily activities."

Raphael noticed the Master's eyes passing over the woman. Then, without being prompted, Jesus called her forward, saying to her, "Woman, you are set free from your infirmity." (Luke 13 v 12) And as he put his hands on her, she straightened up and immediately rejoiced. "Praise the God of the highest heaven that he has mercifully healed me, a frail woman. Praise to the Lord God of heaven and earth. Hallelujah! Praise to our glorious God for freeing me from my affliction." And then, surprisingly, she began to dance. The people around her began to rejoice too, calling out praises to God in loud voices.

But not everybody in that synagogue that day was celebrating. The synagogue ruler, for instance, marched up to Jesus indignantly and cried out to the people in a domineering voice, "There are six days for work. So come and be healed on those days, not on the Sabbath." (Luke 13 v 14)

"You hypocrites!" challenged Jesus. "Doesn't each of you on the Sabbath untie his ox or donkeyfrom the stall and and lead it out to give it water? Then should not this woman, a daughter of Abraham, whom Satan has kept bound for eighteen long years, be set free on the Sabbath day from what bound her?" (Luke 13, vs 15-16)

The synagogue ruler turned aside restlessly, but that didn't stop the eyes of the people from boring into the back of his head. And it didn't stop their delighted chatter as they praised God and kept complimenting Jesus for all the miracles he kept performing.

"This man keeps doing wonderful things."

"Isn't he amazing."

"He heals people all over the place – wherever he goes."

"He opens the eyes of the blind."

"He unstops the mute tongue and makes the deaf hear again."

"Did you know he can even heal lepers."

"And paralysed men."

"But look what he's done for this woman. Who's ever heard of straightening a bent woman up – instantly – at the click of a finger."

"He even has the power to bring dead people back to life."

"He must be an amazing prophet."

"God must love him a lot to bless him so much."

"His healing touch is legendary."

"I know where I'm coming when I get sick."

While Jesus was causing such a stir among the crowds, the Pharisees were mumbling and grumbling amongst themselves. Raphael didn't like what he was hearing. That the 'religious' men of the time could plot a 'man's' death for performing wondrous miracles was beyond his comprehension. Their minds must be so warped and twisted by sin.

Meanwhile, Jesus had exited the synagogue and was strolling, to Raphael's great surprise, towards the house of a Pharisee. It never ceased to amaze him that Jesus moved so freely among all classes of men, the poor and the vulnerable, the wealthy and the rulers. And even those hypocritical Pharisees who gave him so much opposition were graced with his presence in their homes.

But when Jesus was around, the weak and afflicted managed to gain entrance even into the home of a respected Pharisee. Raphael noticed a man who was obviously in great pain in this Pharisee's house. His legs and feet were very swollen and he had difficulty in walking. One of the guests pointed at the sick man and said to his friend, "That man has dropsy. He's going to die soon. He shouldn't even be here. He should be at home praying to God to forgive his many sins; for he must have sinned much, otherwise he wouldn't be so severely afflicted. I'm glad that's not me."

Jesus, who was already reclining at the table, looked around the room. His expression was so authoritative that it wasn't long before every man in that room had turned to him, forgoing their conversation in the hope that they would hear some words of encouragement from the teacher. After all, there were many eminent teachers in that room and they deserved to be enlightened by this man who went throughout Galilee and Judea teaching the rabble. Now it was their turn to be inspired.

But instead, Jesus challenged them with a question: "Is it lawful to heal on the Sabbath or not?" (Luke 14 v 3)

Not one person in the room dared to reply to that challenging question. Nobody was prepared to commit to an answer for fear of making a fool of himself. These Pharisees were so conscious of their image. They wanted everyone to think well of them and were constantly currying favour with their fellow Pharisees and especially with the people.

After waiting a while, Jesus got up, walked over to the man with dropsy and took hold of him. "From this moment, you will be well. Your affliction has left you. Go home now and praise God for what he has done for you."

The healed man looked as if he would burst with joy. He ran out of the room, raising his arms and crying out his praises to heaven. But the Pharisees were not amused. "How dare this man heal on the Sabbath day," they muttered among themselves. "It is not right. He has all the other six days of the week on which to heal. Why does he have to choose the Sabbath?"

Jesus did not stay very long in that home. Raphael noticed with horror that one man actually spat at him as he was departing, but Jesus calmly walked on, holding his head high and focusing on what lay ahead of him. Not only was Raphael impressed with his compassion but also with his dignity, despite all the insults and searing criticism he constantly received from the sons of men – who were so puffed up with their own pride that they were blind to the sufferings of their fellow men.

But right now, Raphael felt like concentrating on Jesus, God's only son who was making such dramatic waves in the world. What an inspiration the Christ was and how richly his every action and deed needed to be broadcast across the skies and celebrated in the heavens. For nothing like these miracles had ever been seen on the earth. And no-one like this God-man had ever walked on the earth.

Chapter Nineteen

Raphael was so energised by what Jesus was doing amongst the sons of men that he felt like trumpeting the news himself instead of writing it down first. But he knew there was a good reason for everything in God's kingdom so he continued to follow his instructions to the letter by recording everything he saw. The next event he witnessed, while not necessarily more amazing than anything he had already seen Jesus do, was nevertheless very special because it involved five thousand men, and that was excluding women and children. And it was also an object lesson about God's provision for his people, especially as it reminded Raphael about how God had graciously met all the needs of the Israelites in the desert.

Again and again, Raphael found himself being awed by Jesus' compassion for the people. When he had just heard the devastating news that John the Baptist had been beheaded, he instructed his disciples to withdraw with him to a quiet place so that he could pray. But the people soon learnt where Jesus was. Messengers sped from town to town, spreading the news of Jesus' whereabouts. So many people ran ahead, meeting Jesus and his disciples as they arrived at that remote place.

With dismay, the disciples saw the very large crowds flocking to Jesus.

"Can't you send these crowds away?" asked one of them.

"No, I must teach these people," replied Jesus, "for they are like sheep without a shepherd."

Then Jesus revealed God's word to them, teaching, explaining and illustrating with parables some of the truths contained in God's holy word.

So fascinated were the people that they didn't seem to notice the hours gliding by. They were still paying attention to every word that Jesus said after many hours of listening intently to him. Raphael noticed that the Master's disciples were standing in a huddle discussing something, worried looks on all their faces. After a while, Philip detached himself from the group and went up to Jesus. Raphael flew a lot closer so that he could hear as well as see the drama as it unfolded. Clearly, Philip was concerned enough about the situation to interrupt the Master's teaching: "Master," he said, "it's late and we're in a remote place. Send the crowds away so that they can buy food for themselves, or they might collapse on the way."

Jesus turned to him and said, "You give them something to eat." (Mark 6 v 37)

Philip looked even more worried now. "Master, it would take eight month's wages to buy food for all these people. Do you really want us to spend that much money on bread and give it to them to eat?"

"How many loaves do you have?" asked Jesus. "Go and see."(Mark 6 v 38)

So the disciples went out amongst the crowd, asking if anyone had brought food. To their dismay, they discovered that nobody had any food except for one small boy.

"Master," said Peter, "here is a boy with five loaves and two small fish."

"Bring them here to me," said Jesus.

Without protesting, the small boy handed over his loaves and fish to the disciple, who presented them to Jesus. Taking the food, Jesus further instructed his disciples: "Tell the people to get into groups of fifties and one hundreds, and to sit down on the grass."

This took some time to organise, but when at last the people were all seated, Jesus looked up to heaven and praised God: "Thank you, Father, for providing food for the people. Thank you that you answer our prayers and that you graciously and continuously care for your people." Then very deliberately, he broke one loaf after another. The disciples, who had collected many empty baskets from the people, now began to fill these baskets with the bread and fish Jesus gave to them to distribute amongst the people.

Apart from the time that Raphael had witnessed manna and quail raining down from heaven on the Israelites in the desert, he had never seen anything like this. The five loaves and the two fish that small boy had sacrificed just kept multiplying. They grew so much that every single person seated on the grass, including all the women and children, ate as much as they wanted to. There were even leftovers. Raphael counted as many as twelve basketfuls of them. This was a sensational miracle indeed: one that he couldn't wait to share with every single angel in the heavenly realms. He got to work with his stylus immediately, forming his signature italic script in the wispy cloud formations. His spirit lifted as he heard the first strains of the trumpeters who were gloriously translating his words into the stirring sounds that would reverberate across the skies for some time to come.

Because of the symbolic nature of this miracle, this time, Raphael took some liberties with the headline. God had given him the gift of being able to express himself in words, so he decided to use alliteration and a metaphor to glorify God's name:

Jesus multiplies manna on the mountain

Early one morning, after Jesus had been given some bad news about the beheading of John the Baptist, he withdrew with his disciples to a remote place. Peace and reflection, however, were to be denied him. For messengers had run to the surrounding towns and villages, informing the people of Jesus' whereabouts.

So when they arrived at the place Jesus had identified as a quiet, remote area for prayer and reflection, already a large crowd was waiting to meet Jesus. There were at least five thousand people, excluding the women and the children.

But instead of sending the crowd away, our compassionate Master, who told his disciples that the people were like sheep without a shepherd, taught them about the word of God.

Then such a spectacular event occurred that it should have left the sons of men in no doubt about the divinity of Jesus. When Philip approached the Master, asking him to send the crowd away so that they could buy food for themselves, our Lord asked if anyone there had food. After a thorough search and many queries, it was discovered that only one small boy had some food: just five loaves and two fish. Even though he must have realised how impossible it was for his small contribution to feed such a vast crowd, he offered up his food to share with someone else. How his heart must have sung when he saw what happened next!

Jesus looked up to heaven, thanking his father for his provision. Then he began to break the bread and the fish, handing it to his disciples to distribute amongst the people. Our glorious God, through his beloved son, Jesus, arranged for the bread and the fish to multiply – and multiply – and multiply. When every single person there – more than five thousand men, excluding the women and children – had eaten and had his fill – the disciples picked up twelve basketfuls of bread and fish. Jehovah Jireh our provider, is indeed a gracious and generous God who deserves all praise and honour. So let us worship and glorify him in humble adoration, never forgetting what a great and powerful, yet compassionate, God we serve.

Raphael
The Heavenly Chronicle

The minute Raphael had completed his article, a stream of shimmering light, like a continuous golden thread, slanted towards him from a distant point in the heavens. Before he could fully comprehend what was happening, his fingers were grabbed by an insistent hand; he felt himself being propelled towards the sky, through the clouds and into the highest heavens.

Just as his spirit was exulting over this new privilege that he had been granted – to be transported into the heavenly realms for a temporary rest from his labours – a golden, shining trumpet was thrust into his hand. He was being given the opportunity of spelling out Jesus' praises in the most awesome possible way. He blew his trumpet with much gusto, his spirit rising with every blast as he gave praise, honour, glory and blessing with every fibre of his being to Jesus Christ, his King of Kings and Lord of Lords.

Throngs of angels circled about him, singing and praising God. Michael, who was watching Raphael from a slight distance as he blew his celebratory blasts, had a radiant smile on his face, a smile which didn't diminish in the slightest when the sounds of the trumpet faded and Raphael finally lowered the instrument from his lips.

"What glorious praise," he said appreciatively, his glowing face bathing Raphael in a golden light as he approached him.

"Aah, it's good to be back in heaven, glorifying the King with the trumpet amidst all the other angels and saints."

"I thought you needed some encouragement – a reminder of what is still in store for you when your task on earth has been completed. But you do realise this has merely been an interlude… a small break between the hustle and bustle of activities taking place on the earth amongst the sons of men."

"I know," he replied. "And I wouldn't want to be away for too long. Not with all the amazing physical and spiritual things that Jesus is doing amongst the sons of men. It's amazing how one extraordinary event just keeps on tumbling into the next one – there appears to be no limit to Jesus' power to heal the sick and to forgive the worst of sins the sons of men have committed." Raphael paused. Then he continued thoughtfully. " I'd better go back to my observation post on the earth... wonderful though this interlude has been."

Michael looked pleased: "You always were such a responsible angel. I knew the Lord could trust you with this mission."

Raphael tried not to let his face glow too much. He was very aware how dangerous pride could be, but it did feel so special to be basking in the compliments of the angel Michael himself.

Quite contentedly, he prepared himself mentally for his swift journey back to the earth.

Chapter Twenty

So, still filled with the heavenly angelic sounds in his ears, Raphael, exulting at the glory of God and inspired by the Holy Spirit, winged his way back to earth to follow the Son of God and record his actions. After the extraordinary miracle of the multiplying of the loaves and fishes, he expected huge crowds to be gathering around Jesus as they praised God and thanked him for his amazing provision. But by the time Raphael had arrived back at the Galilean mountainside, all the crowds had gone home and only Jesus and his disciples were left there. In fact, he was just in time to hear Jesus instructing his men to go ahead of him in the boat to Bethsaida.

After they had left, Jesus went up onto the mountainside and knelt down. Raphael, pleased that Jesus at last had time to be alone with his Father, watched in awe and reverence as Jesus spent the rest of the day on his knees praying. It was already evening when Jesus got up from his knees. Black clouds were gathering and a strong wind was whipping up. Soon it would be dark.

Purposefully, Jesus walked towards the Sea of Galilee. Raphael did wonder where he was going to find another boat at this hour. But he soon realised his error. What need did Jesus, the powerful Son of God, have for a boat? Calmly and with great dignity, he stepped right onto the water and, as if it was hard, strong and stable like solid ground, he began to walk across the churning waters as if they were the firmest, most solid of land surfaces.

Although the boat was already a considerable distance from the land – at least five or six kilometres – the long stretch of water presented no obstacle for Jesus. The Son of Man glided speedily across the water, which by now was choppy and wild. When he got near the disciples' boat, Raphael could see that it was being buffeted by the wind and the waves. All the disciples were clutching onto anything solid they could find. They looked really disturbed, but when they saw the bright, shining man approaching them across the lake, they cried out in fear. "It's a ghost!"

"It's come to punish us."

"It'll sink the boat – and then… "

"We need Jesus to protect us! Why didn't he come with us?"

"He knows how dangerous these Galilean storms can be. He should have come."

"Help! Help!"

But even in the midst of this chaos, Jesus called out to them in a strong, comforting voice, "Take courage. It is I. Don't be afraid." (Matthew 14 v 27) He slowed down his pace and walked with measured steps on the waves so that they wouldn't be scared of him.

"It's the Lord!" cried one of his disciples. "Lord, let me come to you on the water."

"Come Peter," said Jesus, reaching out his arm.

Immediately, Peter began to walk towards Jesus on the water. The other disciples just stared. But then Peter looked down at the violent waves which were about to engulf him. He panicked and began to sink. "Save me, Lord, save me," he cried out.

Jesus reached out his hand and caught him, saying, "You of little faith, why did you doubt?" (Matthew 14 v 31)

As soon as Jesus got into the boat, the wild wind died down and the furious waves subsided. Peter looked at Jesus and said, "Truly, you are the Son of God." (Matthew 14 v 33) Some of the others got down on their knees and began to praise and worship him.

Raphael wanted to sing aloud too, but he knew that wouldn't be wise. He wondered whether these men had any idea just how often they were protected on earth. Of course at this point, they would believe that association with Jesus protected them, but if they delved carefully into the Psalms and listened to his teaching, they would know that although this was certainly true as far as their eternal destinies were concerned, on earth they would have trouble. How often had Raphael heard Jesus exhorting them to take up their crosses and follow him? Did they even know what that meant? Did he, Raphael? Not entirely. He was sent to perform a specific task on the earth and he wanted to do his duty thoroughly. He may understand more about the heavenly realms than these men here in that boat, but he was humbled enough by Jesus' Spirit-filled teachings and awed sufficiently by God the Father, creator and sustainer of the universe, in all his magnificence, to realise that his 'knowledge' was miniscule. He was grateful that he had been considered worthy to perform a task for the Lord.

So while the latest incident was freshly in his mind, he took out his stylus. Only now, after writing all those other articles, had he realised the importance of subheadings. Often, as a novice reporter, he had written extremely bland headings which didn't even begin to describe just how powerful and loving and awesome Jesus was, and just how awesome and miraculous and supernatural his actions on earth had been – and continued to be. Although Raphael was conscious of his limitations, he wanted at least to try and capture some of the qualities his King possessed, and give some sort of inkling of what Jesus meant to him.

So he began to craft the news that would fill the angels and all the other heavenly creatures with unspeakable joy.

Jesus Christ walks on the water
Men acknowledge Jesus as the Son of God

On the Sea of Galilee, Jesus showed his power and his authority over every living thing, including the waters.

At midday, after the crowds who had been taught by Jesus and fed by him in such a miraculous way had dispersed, Jesus instructed his disciples to get into their boat on the Sea of Galilee and go ahead of him to Bethsaida on the other side of the lake. He then went, alone, up on the mountainside for a much-needed and special time of prayer with his Father. By the time he had finished his praying, it was already dark. Wind had come down from the surrounding mountains, whipping up large waves across the Sea of Galilee. But Jesus walked calmly towards the edge of the lake. There were no boats nearby and I wondered how Jesus was going to reach his disciples who were by now a considerable distance from the shore. But of course, I should not have wondered.

Jesus resolutely set foot on the water and began to walk on the churning waters as if they had been as solid as firm ground. He was walking fast across the considerable distance, almost as if he was skimming the surface of the lake.

As he approached the disciples' boat, which was being furiously tossed this way and that by the waves and taking in a substantial amount of water, the men saw our glorious Master on the water and cried out in terror: "It's a ghost." They covered their faces with their arms and trembled in fear. Jesus slowed down his pace and, full of compassion, he stretched out his arm towards them and said, "It is I. Don't be afraid."(John 6 v 20)

The impulsive disciple, Peter, immediately replied, "Lord, if it is you, tell me to come out to you on the lake."

"Come Peter," he said, extending his other arm to his beloved disciple.

Peter actually stepped onto the water and began to walk towards Jesus, but then he looked down, saw the water engulfing him, and began to sink. "Help, Lord, save me," he cried out.

Jesus reached out his hand and pulled Peter up from the churning waters. "You of little faith," he said, "why did you doubt?"(Matthew 14 v 31)

As soon as Jesus and Peter stepped into the boat, the other disciples got down on their knees in worship to their Lord. Wonderfully, Peter recognised who Jesus was: "Truly, you are the

Son of God," (Matthew 15 v 33) he said. There was much rejoicing in that boat on the Sea of Galilee that evening. The power and authority of the Lord had been clearly revealed by Jesus to his followers. This was a special moment on earth which is worth celebrating in the heavens.

Raphael
The Heavenly Chronicle

Hardly had the news been announced in the heavens than the trumpets, stringed instruments, tambourines and cymbals were already sounding out harmonies far above his head. Even from his position here far below on earth, Raphael could hear the beautiful music drifting through the air and encircling the lake. He smiled to himself at the thought of being one of the privileged few down on earth who could actually hear that music. If only the sons of men would open their ears to the music of the heavens! Perhaps then there wouldn't be so much conflict, greed and aggression on the earth that God had made so beautifully and meticulously. But most of them seemed to be so busy indulging themselves with sensuous pleasures and the worries and concerns of this life.

Yet God had graciously broken into the lives of men, sending his very own Son to teach and instruct them, and to show them how to live. He was also, over and over again, graciously demonstrating his power and authority over everything in earth and heaven, so that men might believe in his name. How long was it going to take them to recognise who he was? At least Peter and this small band of disciples were gradually getting the picture. And God obviously had a plan to spread the word through Jesus, and through these men.

It was fascinating to watch his plan unfolding day by day, week by week and year by year. But, as Raphael knew, God's plan spanned more than this finite time: it spanned eternity. How extraordinarily privileged Raphael felt to be a small, in fact a miniscule, part of this great and awesome plan of God.

Chapter Twenty-One

One day, as Jesus was walking through the streets and, as usual, a large crowd was following him, there was a commotion. A dark-skinned, black-haired woman, her hair awry and her arms a-flail, was attempting to get through the crowd to reach Jesus. She was screaming out, "Let me through, let me through. I need to see Jesus. I need to speak to him. Urgently. My daughter is demon-possessed."

The men in the crowd were trying to push her back – to prevent her from causing more of a disturbance – to stop her from approaching Jesus. Even his closest disciples looked thoroughly rattled, for they didn't know what to do with this persistent, screeching woman. But uncharacteristically, Jesus continued on his way, seemingly ignoring the cries of this obviously distressed woman. While Raphael was surprised by the Lord's attitude, he was quite sure that there was a reason for his apparent indifference; that there was a lesson he wanted to teach from this particular example. So he felt relaxed as he watched the drama unfolding. The disciples, however, were anything but calm. They looked thoroughly distressed. "Lord," said one of them, "send this woman away or she won't give us any peace."

"Yes Lord," said another. "What's more, she's a stranger. They say she's a Syro-Phoenician. She's a foreigner in these parts – she shouldn't be allowed to create such a commotion."

Jesus, however, continued walking. By this time, the woman had managed to push herself to the very front of the crowd. Despite the crush, she forced herself right in front of Jesus and knelt at his feet. "Lord," she said desperately, "my daughter is suffering from demon-possession and I know you can help her." Surprisingly, Jesus turned away from her and continued walking. At this, she desperately grabbed his cloak, pulled herself in front of his feet and said, "Lord, you can heal my daughter."

At that Jesus replied, "I was sent only to the lost sheep of Israel… It is not right to take the children's food and toss it to their dogs." (Matthew 15 vs 24,26)

Raphael was amazed that instead of cringing and slinking away into the crowd after an answer like that from the Master, she stayed kneeling, looking up at him with a pleading look in her eyes. "Yes Lord, but even the dogs eat the crumbs that fall from their master's table." (Matthew 15 v 27)

Jesus paused then, turned to her and said, "Woman, you have great faith. Your request is granted." (Matthew 15 v 28)

A glow spread over the woman's face as she got up from the ground and went on her way. Raphael followed her to see what the reaction would be to her daughter's healing. For without a shadow of a doubt, when Jesus said someone was well again, they would, indeed, be well. The woman didn't seem to doubt the Master's word either. With confident, long strides, she was hurrying towards her home. Because this was such a significant moment in this woman's life, Raphael even followed her into her daughter's bedroom. How happy was she to see her daughter sitting up on her bed, 'normal' and in her right mind. Raphael, too, rejoiced at the Master's power over evil spirits and demons. It was a reminder to him that the evil spirits would be decisively defeated, once and for all, at the end times by God the Father, God the Holy Spirit and by Jesus, God's son.

What a wonderful moment this was for Raphael, particularly as he remembered the fierce battle that had raged in the heavens when that arrogant angel, Satan, had gathered his armies in an attempt to defeat the mighty King of the Ages. Nobody could contend with the Lord and win the battle. All his enemies would be defeated – forever – for all eternity. Raphael couldn't wait for that great day of judgement to arrive.

He didn't reflect for too long on that final day of judgement. Instead, as usual, he hurried to spread the news about God's Son defeating the enemy, Satan, here on earth.

The Christ extends his healing powers beyond the lost sheep of Israel

A woman was shrieking and waving her arms at Jesus as the crowds followed him as usual along the road. Because the appearance of this woman was very different from the locals, the people began asking about her. It was established by one of the disciples that she was from Syro-Phoenicia, but as this foreigner had clearly heard about Jesus and his healing powers, she remained absolutely determined to present her request to him despite all the opposition she was encountering.

Some of the men shook their fists at her, women were grumbling amongst themselves about the huge din she was kicking up, and even the children were whining about her. At last, when he could tolerate the commotion no longer, and seeing that the crowd was becoming restless, one of Jesus' disciples went up to him and said, "Master, send that woman away or she will give us no peace." But Jesus, much to the consternation of the disciple, continued to walk on, ignoring the cries of the wild woman. "Master," said the disciple more urgently, "this woman is causing a disturbance. Send her away." Still, Jesus walked forward, not even turning to look at the woman, who by now was pushing and shoving everyone in her path, so determined was she to get to Jesus.

When, finally, she had forced herself to the front of the crowd, she flung herself at the Master's feet. "Sir, my daughter is possessed by a demon. I know you can heal her."

Jesus took yet another step forward, away from the distressed woman. But she clung to his robe. "Teacher, please will you heal my daughter."

Now Jesus did turn to look down at her. "I was sent only to the lost sheep of Israel. It is not right to take the children's bread and toss it to their dogs." (Matthew 15 vs 24, 26)

"Yes Lord, but even the dogs eat the crumbs that fall from their masters' table." (Matthew 15 v 27)

Jesus' expression just then was one of compassion and understanding:
"Woman, you have great faith! Your request is granted. "

All the shouting, crying out and begging stopped immediately. The woman let go of Jesus' robe, picked herself off the ground and calmly walked away.

Knowing that Jesus had healed the woman's daughter of demon possession but wanting to see her reaction when she got home, I, together with a number of other curious onlookers, followed the woman home. The crowd waited outside, but I had the privilege of going with her right into her daughter's bedroom. I witnessed the woman's sheer delight and relief as she saw that her daughter was sitting up on her bed, dressed modestly and talking to her mother with respect. I left after the woman had taken her daughter in her arms and hugged her, weeping tears of joy and praising the Lord.

In this wonderful demonstration of God's grace and compassion, Jesus is showing insiders and outsiders just how strong his healing power is, and just how much authority he has over the evil and the dark forces of this world.

Raphael
The Heavenly Chronicle

As Jesus continued to walk along the dusty road, Raphael noticed that he was looking tired. His many encounters with people, and especially the healings, must be taking a great deal of energy. The Son of God on earth, despite the awesome power which the Father gave him, was subject to all the physical weaknesses that man suffered. Jesus was therefore already leading his disciples to a remote place on the Galilean mountainside in the obvious hope that he would be able to teach them quietly. But of course, wherever Jesus went, the crowds followed. Judging by the number of people following

Jesus, Raphael doubted that the Master would get his time of respite. But as the good shepherd, he would never turn those lost sheep away. Rather, he would feed them, both physically, miraculously and metaphorically. Raphael watched and followed in awe to see what would happen next.

Chapter Twenty-Two

Raphael only stopped flying when Jesus had, indeed, reached that Galilean mountainside. There, he listened to Jesus patiently teaching the crowds for many hours which spilled over into days. But Jesus did something else remarkable on that mountainside. As, from there, Raphael watched the events unfold beneath him, he was powerfully reminded of God's provision and his graciousness. Jesus was providing the people, yet again, with a graphic object lesson in who he was.

For three days already on that remote mountainside, far away from the villages and towns, he had been teaching all who had followed him there, including the lame, the blind, the crippled and the mute. It had gladdened Raphael's heart to hear the people cry out in praise to God and lift their hands in adoration to their Father as they listened to Jesus opening his mouth in parables. But just as had happened the last time, his disciples were concerned about physical needs. One of them approached him and said, "Teacher, send these people away to buy food, or they will collapse with hunger." Jesus turned to him and commanded, "Go and see how much food the people have."

"Teacher, we have already done that," he replied, a touch of frustration in his tone, "but we have only managed to find seven loaves of bread and a few fish amongst all these people."

Jesus looked him directly in the eye and said with great authority, "Arrange the people into groups of fifties and one hundreds and get them to sit down."

Although the disciples followed Jesus' instructions, they were muttering among themselves, and were clearly worried and concerned. How could they fail to remember what Jesus had done before? Very recently, on this very same Galilean mountainside, Jesus had miraculously fed more than five thousand people. Did they still not believe in the power of God? Did they not remember their Lord raining the bread of heaven on the hot desert sand? And now his son, the Christ, was multiplying bread for them to eat. Was it that they still didn't believe Jesus was God's son? Why were they so slow to open their eyes? To unstop their ears? Why were they so blind and so deaf? Raphael decided to concentrate his attention on Jesus and not on the people with hearts of stone and the understanding of brutish beasts.

Jesus patiently waited till the crowd was seated, then, holding up the bread and the fish to heaven, he gave thanks to his father, blessed the food and passed it to his disciples. When the disciples distributed the food, they found that all the people – more than four thousand of them – ate and were satisfied. What's more, there were seven basketfuls of food left over. The people were amazed and praised God, but Raphael found himself wondering just how long those praises would be on the peoples' lips. These fickle people appeared to have very short memories! Of course, he knew who would sing and shout sustained praises to God for his mighty and miraculous acts of power: his colleagues in the heavenly realms, throngs upon throngs of angelic beings. But before he could get to work with his stylus, he noticed that Jesus and his disciples were taking off in a boat from Magadan. Twice before, Raphael had witnessed Jesus calming the storm as he instructed the winds and the waves to die down, and once before he had actually seen Jesus walking on the wild water. So he decided he wasn't going to miss out on any of the action now. For a long time, he hovered over the boat, closely watching its progress across this vast sea. At long last, he saw that it was approaching Caesarea Philippi. As soon as he got to shore, Raphael noticed that Jesus was seeking out a quiet place to rest. When Jesus sat down in a quiet, sheltered spot along the beach, his disciples clustered around him on the sand.

But Raphael should have known better. Jesus didn't want to rest – when did he ever find the time to rest when he had more important things to do, like teaching his disciples about himself? Jesus began with a direct question: "Who do people say the Son of Man is?" (Matthew 16 v 13) All the disciples seemed to be talking at the same time in their confusion, but one of them managed to be heard above the others: "They say you're John the Baptist come to life again." This got the attention of the others, who quietened down after that.

"I've heard some people saying that Elijah has come back," said one of them thoughtfully.

"Really. I heard a whole group of men insisting that you were Jeremiah, the prophet, come back to earth."

When he heard all this, Jesus looked at them challengingly: "But what about you? Who do you say that I am?"

Immediately, Simon Peter went to kneel at his feet: "You are the Christ, the Son of the living God." (Matthew 16 v 16)

Jesus extended his arm and placed his hand on Peter's head: "Blessed are you, Simon, son of Jonah, for this was not revealed to you by man, but by my Father in heaven. And I tell you that you are Peter, and on this rock I will build my church, and the gates of Hades will not overcome it."(Matthew 16 vs 17-18)

What an extraordinary privilege and amazing responsibility Jesus was giving to this Peter. Raphael was sure the man hadn't understood the full impact or meaning of his Master's words. In fact, he looked, if anything, rather bewildered and confused. But his expression changed suddenly to one of respect and adoration as he gazed into the eyes of his Lord and Master. Raphael, once again, felt elated that at least one of Jesus' disciples recognised Jesus for who he was: the Son of the living God. He also had a pressing urge to share the good news with the angels – and to pass on the message of Christ's miraculous provision, yet again, of food for the people.

So, with joy in his heart, he began to compose his article.

Jesus multiplies bread, whilst Peter acknowledges God's Son

Late one afternoon, on the Galilean mountainside, Jesus once again demonstrated to the people who he was. By performing another mighty miracle, he showed the people that, as God's son, he had the power to multiply bread and fish.

Just as God the Father rained down the bread of angels from heaven on the Israelites in the wilderness, so Jesus kept breaking bread and multiplying it so that more than four thousand people could eat their fill and be satisfied. The multitude praised God for this mighty miracle.

Later that day, when the crowd had dispersed, Jesus took his disciples aside and questioned them about who people said he was. They replied with the names of well-known prophets: John the Baptist, Elijah, Jeremiah. But Jesus was more interested in hearing about who they, his own disciples, thought he was. So he asked them, "But who do you say that I am?"

It was Simon Peter who, very thrillingly, replied, "You are the Christ, the Son of the living God." (Matthew 16 v 16)

Jesus turned to him and said, "Blessed are you, Simon son of Jonah, for this was not revealed to you by man, but by my Father in heaven. And I tell you that you are Peter, and on this rock, I will build my church, and the gates of Hades will not overcome it." (Matthew 16 vs 17-18)

The Lord has revealed that he has a plan to build his church upon the earth. We need to celebrate miracles like the multiplying loaves and fish, but we also need to celebrate the spreading of God's word amongst the sons of men and the expansion of his church through all countries and to the ends of the earth.

Raphael
The Heavenly Chronicle

The minute the trumpets announced this wonderful news in the heavenly realms, a new song was being created by the generators of musical scores and the lyricists. So efficient and eager were they that almost instantaneously, the choir masters and conductors were gathering a multitude of angels in the skies so that collectively, they could make a joyful noise unto the Lord. Raphael, in eager anticipation of the jubilant sounds that were shortly to be exploding across the heavens, lifted himself to a good vantage point. There, hovering a little way above the earth, he could just see the shapes of men like tiny miniature toys far below him. Although he was unable to see the magnificent choral and orchestral extravaganza that was being trumpeted forth to every corner of the heavens, he could hear the sounds better from here. And strictly speaking, he was not disobeying any of Michael's instructions about observing Jesus' ministry to the sons of men on earth. From his position in the sky, he could see if there were any significant movements of those miniature people far below him. And as he had learnt by now, where the crowds were, there Jesus was.

Soon, he was immersing himself in the exquisite sounds: although all the praise was lyrically harmonious, today he was particularly impressed by the purity of the young treble voices. To hear young voices lifted in adoration to the King of Kings and Lord of Lords always moved him deeply, chiefly because of the origins of these choirs. These were not originally angelic choirs: these were the choirs of the saints. Born of the sons of men, these boys had died young. They had such beautiful voices that they were immediately co-opted into the heavenly choirs, and not one angel regretted it. They made a really special addition to the swelling ranks of the heavenly choirs chiefly because of the cleanness and innocence of their voices. To listen to them for just a few minutes was to transport you immediately into an innocent place before the entry of sin and death into the world. And to listen to them for extended periods was to believe that mankind could be redeemed for all eternity.

But at the very moment that Raphael was being transported into the heavenly realms, Jesus' closest disciples were about to experience a stunning display of God's glory revealed only to them, the chosen few.

Chapter Twenty-Three

Raphael was watching particularly carefully as Jesus advanced with intent towards a remote mountain with his three closest disciples, Peter, James and John. It seemed to Raphael fairly obvious that he was looking for a quiet place to be alone with his disciples. Perhaps he was going to reveal something special about his father to them, or he could just want to pray together with them. Somehow, though, Raphael felt a great sense of anticipation, as if he was about to witness an extraordinary event. So he made sure that his attention was completely focused on the four as they began to climb the mountain. Not even the exquisite notes of a distant harp were going to distract him from his mission: to observe carefully and to record accurately the extremely significant event he was convinced he was about to witness.

It began with Jesus kneeling down and praying. His disciples were clustered around him; just as they, also, began to pray, Raphael saw that Jesus' glory was being displayed on the earth; just as God revealed himself to Moses through the burning bush, so God was revealing Jesus to his disciples by transforming him radically in order to display his glory.

As Jesus was praying, Raphael noticed that his clothes were glowing: they were as white as light, or as glowing as a flash of lightning. James, pointing to Jesus, mumbled, "We could never, ever bleach anything so white; look what's happening to our Lord."

The light was so bright that the three disciples had to shield their eyes to stop it from blinding them. Jesus, however, got up and walked a little higher up the mountain where Moses and Elijah, in all their glorious splendour, were waiting for him. Jesus spoke to them about his forthcoming departure which he said was about to happen at Jerusalem. They discussed the significance of this event.

Meanwhile, the disciples, who had been rubbing their eyes in a daze, suddenly became fully awake. Peter stared at the three figures before him. Clearly, he could hardly believe what he was witnessing: that Jesus, Moses and Elijah were all right in front of him on this mountainside talking to each other was beyond belief. A broad smile broke across Peter's face as Raphael watched the brilliant celestial light that bathed the bodies of Jesus, Moses and Elijah filtering across to Peter, who impulsively walked up to Jesus and said, "Lord, it is good for us to be here. If you wish, I will put up three shelters – one for you, one for Moses and one for Elijah." (Matthew 17 v 4)

Before he had even finished speaking, a huge white shining cloud descended from heaven and surrounded them. Suddenly, a deep, rich voice, the voice of the Lord God himself, began to speak from the cloud: "This is my Son, whom I love; with him I am well pleased. Listen to him!" (Matthew 17 v 5)

The reaction from the disciples was immediate. Raphael watched them falling to the ground, trembling and terrified. But after Moses and Elijah had been taken up into heaven again, Jesus calmly walked over to the disciples and touched each one of them in turn.

"Get up. Don't be afraid," he said to them. When the disciples looked up, there was only Jesus standing there.

"Come, let us go," he said.

As they were following him down the mountainside, he said, "Don't tell anyone what you have seen, until the Son of Man has been raised from the dead." (Matthew 17 v 9)

Raphael felt a wonderful sense of elation stirring within him at Jesus' words, but Peter, clearly not understanding what Jesus had just said to him, asked, "Why then do the teachers of the law say Elijah must come first?"

Jesus replied, "To be sure, Elijah comes and will restore all things. But I tell you, Elijah has already come and they did not recognise him, but have done to him everything they wished. In the same way, the Son of Man is going to suffer at their hands." (Matthew 17 vs 11-12)

"Oh, you mean John the Baptist," said Peter.

"He is the Elijah I speak of," affirmed Jesus.

Yet none of them asked him about the Son of Man suffering in the hands of the people. These sons of men had very limited insight, if any understanding at all, about the plan of God as it was unfolding on earth. But Raphael realised that even he, as a privileged celestial being, had not been given complete insight into the final and perfect plan of God. As an obedient servant and messenger, he was there to carry out, bit by bit, his instructions; he was a very small cog in a giant wheel; he felt very excited to be part of the body of created beings who were called to advance God's kingdom in this world and the next. And the fact that his particular task spanned two worlds, the earth and the heavens, made it all the more fulfilling.

He had just witnessed one of the most glorious events of Jesus' ministry on earth; with great enthusiasm, he began to compose the article that would result in instrumental and sung praises reverberating across the heavens for many days to come.

A transfigured Jesus meets Moses and Elijah

Near the top of a Galilean mountain where Jesus had gone to pray with his closest disciples Peter, James and John, God revealed the glory of his Son to the sons of men.

It happened that while Jesus was praying, his clothes became as bright as white-hot lightning and his face shone like the sun. When he got up, Moses and Elijah approached him. They began to converse about his imminent departure from the earth.

Peter did not understand the significance of what he was witnessing. He went up to Jesus and said, "Lord, it is good for us to be here. If you like, I will put up three shelters, one for you, one for Moses and one for Elijah."(Matthew 17 v 4)

At that moment, a huge white cloud descended from heaven and enveloped them all. As the deep, authoritative voice of God began to speak from the midst of the cloud, the disciples fell down, terrified. "This is my Son, whom I love; with him I am well pleased. Listen to him."

211

(Matthew 17 v 5) The terrified men were too scared to look up. Shaking violently, they remained on the ground.

But Jesus, filled with compassion, touched each of them in turn. "Get up. Don't be afraid," (Matthew 17 v 6) he said.

One by one, the disciples got up. They were all still trembling but they did manage to follow him down the mountainside. As he was walking, he turned to them and said, "Don't tell anyone what you have seen, until the Son of Man has been raised from the dead." (Matthew 17 v 9) All three men looked confused, but they said nothing.

As with Moses from the burning bush and the descending dove at Jesus' baptism, the Father, in transfiguring his son, has clearly revealed Christ's glory. Oh, that men would open their eyes to see it.

Raphael
The Heavenly Chronicle

This time, before the news of Jesus' transfiguration had been trumpeted across the entire heavens, many of the angels had already heard the news from the returning Moses and Elijah. The masses of angels who welcomed them into the heavenly realms were already warming up their voices and tuning their instruments. The momentous revelation that the sons of men had witnessed was worth celebrating. Surely, after this magnificent display of God's glory, men would want to draw closer to Jesus. So jubilant was this group of angels when they heard about Jesus' transfiguration on the earth that many of them, to the accompaniment of multiple instruments, began to move their bodies in a graceful dance. Their uplifted hands and arms made repetitive triangles of praise; the intricate patterns they were making with their legs and feet suggested that their joy was overflowing; and their flapping wings added much energy and excitement to their dance as they propelled themselves from one corner of the widening dance space to another.

Raphael, although he couldn't participate in these particular celebrations, was witnessing another much more humble, but nevertheless deeply stirring, tribute to King Jesus on earth from the sons of men.

Chapter Twenty-Four

After witnessing so many wonderful miracles and listening to all Jesus was teaching, Raphael would have expected all mankind from the region that Jesus had been frequenting to be praising the Son of God with the angels, and to be bowing down to worship him. He was surprised by all the opposition the Christ was experiencing from the sons of men, particularly from the religious leaders like the Pharisees and the Sadducees. How could their eyes be so blind when they scrutinised the law so meticulously? Yet they deliberately turned themselves away from the Son of God, effectively barring themselves from life.

When Raphael had first been assigned his mission of recording events for the angels, the last thing he had expected was resistance and hostility from the very beings on earth who had been created by God. And now, in his great compassion and generosity and at great sacrifice to himself, he had sent his only son to save all people who came to him from their sins, and to figuratively open their eyes and unstop their ears. But they obstinately insisted on remaining in their sins, and persisted in choosing blindness and deafness.

Which was why Raphael's spirit was greatly uplifted when he witnessed crowds of men, women and children praising the son of David with 'Hallelujahs' as they enthusiastically waved palm branches in the air or lined the road with them. He had been watching Jesus and his disciples closely as they approached Jerusalem, where lately there had been a groundswell of opposition building up against the Son of God. Raphael found himself being extremely concerned about Jesus as he approached the holy city where his enemies lay waiting for him. In his travels, he had heard all the intense discussions and vicious plots to trap Jesus in his words and even to kill him. But he knew he daren't interfere with God's plan for his son; that he couldn't intervene and that he would just have to be an inert witness to whatever took place on the earth below him.

Jesus had now arrived at Bethphage on the Mount of Olives. Raphael heard him giving clear instructions to two of his disciples: "Go to the village ahead of you, and at once you will find a donkey tied there, with her colt by her. Untie them and bring them to me. If anyone says anything to you, tell him that the Lord needs them, and he will send them right away." (Matthew 21, vs 2-3)

Raphael could feel the buzz of excitement building up inside him as his Lord and Master was speaking. He was mindful of the prophecy of Zechariah that was about to be fulfilled in front of his very eyes:

"See, your king comes to you,

righteous and having salvation,

gentle and riding on a donkey,

on a colt, the foal of a donkey." (Zechariah 9 v9)

With great anticipation, he watched the disciples going to do exactly as Jesus had instructed them. As Jesus had said, the donkey and the colt were handed over freely – no questions were asked and there was no opposition.

When the disciples brought the donkey and colt to Jesus, they placed their cloaks on them; as soon as Jesus had taken his seat, the disciples began to lead him down to Jerusalem. The people immediately began to gather around this little procession: the closer they got to Jerusalem, the more the crowd swelled. As they saw Jesus approaching, the people spread their cloaks on the road in front of him. Some of them cut branches from the trees and spread them in the road; others exultantly waved their branches, crying out in loud voices, "Hosanna to the Son of David."

"Blessed is he who comes in the name of the Lord."

"Blessed is the coming kingdom of our father David."

"Hosanna in the highest." (Matthew 21 v 9)

In his heart, Raphael was joining in the crowd's celebrations. How uplifting it was to hear the Son of God praised and honoured as he ought to be. It was only a few days later, when Raphael reflected on this incident, that he realised how shallow the praise of these people was; that Jesus, the humble, suffering servant, was not the Messiah they were expecting. They were looking, rather, for a warrior king, someone with the authority and the power to free them from the oppressive shackles of Rome. Whipped up by the Pharisees, this same crowd of people who were singing 'Hosannas' to the King would viciously turn against him, seeking his death.

But right now, it seemed that the whole of Jerusalem was bursting with curiosity and praise for the man entering the holy city on a donkey. Many people were asking who this man was. Those who thought they were in the know replied, "This is Jesus, the prophet from Nazareth in Galilee."

If only they had opened their eyes a little wider, they could have seen who this really was who was riding on a humble colt into Jerusalem.

However, the unexpected praise of these sons of men was certainly worth recording and celebrating. So Raphael, as usual, began to pen his article which was simultaneously trumpeted into the four corners of the heavens.

Jesus is praised with 'Hosannas' by the sons of men

In fulfilment of Zechariah's prophecy, Jesus was riding into Jerusalem on a donkey from Bethphage on the Mount of Olives. His disciples had lain their cloaks on the donkey and its colt and were leading their Master into the Holy City in the build-up to holy week.

The closer he got to Jerusalem, the more the crowds gathered. The people were cutting branches from the palm trees and lining the road with them. Others were waving their palm branches in the air. All of them were shouting their praises to the Son of David as Jesus passed by. Some of the loud cries that rent the air were: "Hosanna to the Son of David!"

"Blessed is he who comes in the name of the Lord!"

"Hosanna in the highest!" (Matthew 21, v 9)

The excitement in the air was palpable, especially amongst Jesus' disciples who were clearly enjoying the spectacle, and relishing all the adulation their Master was receiving. With the adoring crowd singing their praises to the Son of David, they were obviously finding it exhilarating to be associated with Jesus. They all had broad smiles on their faces and some of them were waving enthusiastically at the crowd.

Raphael
The Heavenly Chronicle

But Jesus, turning his head neither to the right nor to the left, rode resolutely on towards Jerusalem, a set expression on his face. Undoubtedly, he was focusing on the difficult mission ahead of him, determined as he was to complete the work God had assigned to him, thereby carrying out the plan of God for the whole world.

As soon as the news was trumpeted to them, the creative angels began to mimic the celebratory scene on the earth below. This time, to the musical accompaniment and choral renditions of the 'Hosannas' and cries of joy to the Son of David, they used branches from the tree of life itself to wave their praises across the heavens. Almost as if they knew that a change was about to happen in this very crowd's attitude towards Jesus, they made sure that their celebrations lasted much longer than the previous ones. They rejoiced in the temporary adulation the Christ was receiving from the sons of men, knowing full well – from prophecy and the scriptures – that the earthly fortunes of the Son of Man would soon be turning, and that every joyous Hallelujah in heaven was proof that at least they, the celestial beings, would worship and adore Christ the King both now and for all eternity.

Chapter Twenty-Five

Raphael went ahead of Jesus to the temple because he knew that was where his Lord and Master would be going. He was expecting that the people would be praising him all the way to the temple.

Because of the build-up to the Passover, the temple was much more crowded than usual. There were queues of people pushing and shoving as they lined up to buy their obligatory sacrifices. The dove sellers were charging exorbitant rates, whilst some of them who were more desperate to make sales were crying out in loud voices, "Two for the price of one. Bargain doves for sale. Get your sacrifices here. " In some cases, competition for sales was becoming ugly. "Out of my way," Raphael heard one dove seller cry out in a loud voice. "Keep to your own territory. This is my bench." Some of the men were arguing with the money-changers. "This is ridiculous," said a bearded man who was wearing a long robe. "These rates are ludicrously high." But the money-changer insisted on his price. "Get your money somewhere else then. But don't blame me if you get charged higher rates. I'm the most reasonable in the whole of the temple precinct. Unless you want to go to the other side of the city, you won't find a better rate." With bad grace, the man who had been arguing slammed his money down on the table.

Raphael began to feel wildly unsettled. The area below him was turning into the worst kind of market place, with men haggling with each other about prices, the vendors dishonestly cheating the people and the 'customers' feeling so hard done by that they were lashing out against each other. And this was in the forecourt of the temple! What did the sons of men think they were doing in the house of God? Especially in holy week. What would Jesus think about this when he made his triumphal entry into his father's house?

Raphael didn't have to wait very long to find out. As soon as he arrived at the temple and saw what was going on, Jesus was filled with righteous anger. He stormed up to the dove sellers and overturned their benches and the tables of the money changers. Money was scattering across the floor, but the people were so shocked that they did nothing except stare, their mouths agape. Jesus cried out in a loud, angry voice, "It is written. My house will be called a house of prayer, but you are making it a den of robbers." (Matthew 21 v 13)

Instead of advancing into the temple, he turned on his heels and marched away, his disciples trying to keep up with him as he raced down the hill. In fact, so disgusted was he by what he had seen that he just kept walking at quite a pace, right out of the city and all the way to Bethany to the house of Simon the leper. There, he had some respite as his feet were washed, he was welcomed into the house and given a place to recline at the table.

Almost as soon as he had sat down, a woman came right up to him. She was carrying an alabaster jar. She lifted it and poured the contents over Jesus' head. The fragrance of the perfume was so sweet and so strong that it filled the room.

Immediately, those nearby who had seen what this woman had done began to criticise her.

"That's very expensive perfume," said one man. "Why is she wasting it like this?"

"Yes," said another. "The perfume in that jar was worth more than a year's wages. It could have been sold and the money given to the poor."

"And Jesus didn't stop her! Does he even know who this woman is… what a great sinner she is!" One man accused the woman directly: "How can you be so outrageously extravagant – and wasteful? You should be ashamed of yourself."

Now Jesus intervened.

"Why are you bothering this woman?" he said. "She has done a beautiful thing to me. The poor you will always have with you, but you will not always have me. When she poured this perfume on my body, she did it to prepare me for burial. I tell you the truth, wherever the gospel is preached throughout the world,what she has done will also be told, in memory of her." (Matthew 26 vs 10-13)

Then, looking straight at her, he said, "Go in peace. Your faith has saved you." She bowed humbly before him and retreated with her alabaster jar, looking gratefully over her shoulder at Jesus who had forgiven her sins.

Raphael was so outraged by the greed and entitlement that the money changers and dove sellers had demonstrated at the temple that he completely understood his Lord's righteous anger. And he was so moved by the beautiful thing that humble and adoring woman had done for Jesus that he was soon to announce her action to his colleagues in the heavenly realms. For a change, he decided to write an article which contrasted the good and the bad things he had just witnessed. So, carefully choosing his words, he began to pen his article.

Jesus displays righteous anger and commends a beautiful act

After his triumphant entry into Jerusalem, Jesus went straight to the temple. He discovered crowds of people queuing to buy their sacrifices, whilst disgruntled men were haggling about the money changers' exorbitant rates. So incensed was he at this crass commercialism in his father's house that he angrily overturned the tables of the money changers and upset the benches of the dove sellers, crying out in a loud voice, "My house shall be called a house of prayer, but you are making it a den of robbers." (Matthew 21 v 13) He turned on his heels and marched out of the temple, leaving the people confused and gaping.

Jesus walked far that day – as far as Bethany, where Simon the leper welcomed him into his home. It was there, while he was reclining at the table, that a woman did a beautiful thing for him: as Jesus put it, she anointed his body for burial. She poured the contents of an alabaster jar which contained an expensive perfume onto his head. The people criticised her for what they deemed to be an outrageous waste. They knew the value of that perfume; it was worth a year's wages, yet this sinful woman had liberally poured it on Jesus' head. They angrily pointed out that the perfume could have been sold and the money given to the poor.

At this point, Jesus came to the woman's defence: "The poor you will always have with youbut you will not always have me. When she poured this perfume on my body, she did it to prepare me for burial." (Matthew 26 vs 10-13) Jesus continues to expose the motives of the rich and influential, but to commend those who have a genuine heart for God. In so doing, he demonstrates that he is the king of the whole earth and the heavens; that he is a righteous yet compassionate judge who knows the secrets of men's hearts.

Raphael
The Heavenly Chronicle

The angels' praise for the King of creation was incredibly intense that day. They celebrated the Christ, the Messiah, with rich trumpet calls, with the crashing of cymbals, with sincere, heartfelt cries of 'Hosanna to the King', and with the blended harmonies of multitudinous cries.

They knew now that the Son of God would be tested almost beyond his endurance; that he would experience great physical and mental suffering and that he would be brutally separated from his father. So they ensured that this particular celebration would be heard loudly, and have a great impact on even celestial beings in distant corners of the heavens.

Soon, for a brief interlude – which would seem to drag on endlessly – the Son of God would be subjected to the worst pain and suffering men knew how to administer. With the ignominy of the sins of the whole world loaded onto him and the deep-seated anguish of being separated from his father, he would suffer like no human being had ever suffered before or would ever suffer again.

Raphael wished, more than ever, to return to the heavens now so that he wouldn't have to witness his Lord and Master's agony, but he knew the only honourable thing to do was to fulfil his task and continue his work till it was completed, just as Jesus was bracing himself to do.

Chapter Twenty-Six

As they approached Jerusalem, Raphael noticed that Jesus was talking earnestly to Peter and John, so he got closer in order to hear what he was talking about. Peter asked the Master, "Where do you want to celebrate the Passover meal?"

Jesus answered him, "Go into the city, and a man carrying a water jar will meet you Follow him. Say to the owner of the house he enters, 'The Teacher asks: Where is my guest room, where I may eat the Passover with my disciples? He will show you a large upper room, furnished and ready. Make preparations for us there." (Mark 14,vs 13-15)

Raphael, when he flew into the city with Jesus' disciples, wasn't at all surprised to observe that everything happened just as Jesus had said it would. When evening came, he was gladdened by the sight of all twelve of his disciples gathering in the room to eat the Passover meal with Jesus. What a beautiful intimate setting for this special feast. Here in this upper room their host had so graciously given them, they would be undisturbed and could enjoy this memorable meal with Jesus.

At the beginning of this special Passover meal, it was with great surprise that Raphael saw that Jesus, instead of reclining at the table and being waited on, got up, took a towel and wrapped it around his tunic, then got down on his knees. This action of Jesus, Raphael realised, was going to change the way the people of God viewed leadership. Taking a bowl of water, he began to wash the first disciple's feet. Before he reached Peter, however, this impulsive disciple protested in a loud voice, "Lord, you will never wash my feet."

"Peter, Peter," said Jesus, compassion filling his eyes, "unless I wash you, you have no part with me."(John 13 v 8)

"Then Lord," Peter replied, "not just my feet, but my hands and head as well."

"A person who has had a bath needs only to wash his feet. His whole body is clean. And you are clean, though not every one of you." (John 13 v 10)

When Jesus got back to his place, he taught them about the significance of what they had just witnessed: "Do you understand what I have done for you? You call me 'Teacher' and 'Lord', and rightly so, for that is what I am. Now that I, your Lord and Teacher, have washed your feet, you also should wash one another's feet. I have set you an example that you should do as I have done for you. I tell you the truth, no servant is greater than his master, nor is a messenger greater than the one who sent him. Now that you know these things, you will be blessed if you do them." (John 13 vs 12-17)

What an extraordinary example the Christ was setting for his disciples. Raphael was truly humbled as he watched Jesus' servanthood in action. What other ruler or teacher would humble himself in this way? The Pharisees and Sadducees lorded themselves over the people, who were expected to defer to them and respect them, even though their behaviour was often not worthy of respect. The Roman procurators, consuls, kings and emperors demanded subservience from their subjects and the people they had conquered. Disobeying their flawed, often unfair, illogical man-made laws, and failure to show respect to those in authority, often resulted in great suffering and even a brutal death. Many a Roman cross with the body of a 'rebel' had been erected alongside busy roads to remind the people who was in control, and to warn them of the horrible fate that awaited them should they oppose the rules of the Roman authorities. In fact, no Jewish priest or Roman ruler had ever, or would ever, be likely to 'debase' himself, thereby showing 'weakness' in front of his subjects. Their type of rule was all about absolute power and domination. Yet Jesus, the Christ, the Messiah, the chosen one of God, his very own son and the king of the whole world, was prepared to humble himself by washing his followers' feet, thereby setting them a simple but inspiring example of how they should live.

When Jesus had finished washing his disciples' feet, he put on his own clothes and went back to his place. Looking around at all the twelve men gathered there, he said, "I have eagerly desired to eat this Passover with you before I suffer. For I tell you, I will not eat it again until it finds fulfilment in the kingdom of God." (Luke 20, vs 15-16)

Raphael's heart contracted. The last meal! The calm before the storm. Immense physical and mental suffering. But looking at those men's faces, he was convinced that not one of them really understood what Jesus was saying to them.

Immediately after this, Jesus said something that shocked them: "I tell you the truth, one of you is going to betray me." (John 13 v 21)

They were horrified. "Surely not me, Lord?" asked one man after another.

"It is the one to whom I will give this piece of bread when I have dipped it in the dish." (John 13 v 26)

Raphael could clearly see the betrayer, Judas Iscariot, dipping his hand into that bowl. Yet the others were so disturbed about the idea of a betrayer being in their very midst – amongst the inner circle of Jesus' trusted disciples – that they didn't seem to notice. Jesus looked directly at Judas and said, "Go and do what you have to."

The others did not appear to be unduly worried about Jesus' command. After all, Judas, as their treasurer, was in charge of the money bags. Perhaps he was going to distribute some of the money amongst the poor.

Judas left the room, and although Raphael wanted to see what he got up to, at this point, all his attention was focused on Jesus and the eleven as he ate his last meal with them. Jesus took up a loaf of bread, gave thanks and broke it. As he passed it around, he said, "This is my body given for you. Do this in remembrance of me." (Luke 22 v 19) Then he took the cup of wine, drank from it and passed it on. "Thiscup is the new covenant in my blood," he said, "which is poured out for you" (Luke 22, v20)

When they had all eaten the bread and drunk the wine, they began to sing a hymn. Then Jesus said, "Come. We must go to the Mount of Olives."

As they were dispersing, Raphael decided he had better check up on Judas. But first he must send news to the heavens about the groundbreaking Passover meal. He didn't have much time. He knew Judas would be making his way towards the temple. So he would have to report very quickly what had happened in the upper room. The betrayer had already achieved what he wanted to, and Jesus had very little time left before his severe trials would begin. So without wasting any time, he got out his stylus and composed his report.

The last Passover marked by servant leadership

In a large upper room in Jerusalem, Jesus shared his last Passover meal with his twelve disciples. But before they even began the meal, he demonstrated his servant leadership by washing each one of his disciples' feet. He used this action of his as an object lesson, showing his followers with a practical example how they should treat one another.

When he had finished, he went back to his place so that they could begin their meal. It was soon evident that this was going to be the most significant Passover meal in all of history. Jesus began by saying, "I have eagerly desired to eat this Passover meal with you before I suffer. I will not eat it again until it finds fulfilment in the kingdom of God." (Luke 20 vs 15-16) Evidently, the disciples did not understand what he was saying to them, as they calmly began to eat of the Passover meal. Until Jesus said to them, "I tell you the truth, one of you is going to betray me." (John 13 v 21)Then there were flustered cries of, "Surely it is not I, Lord." Jesus replied, "It is the one to whom I will give this piece of bread when I have dipped it in the dish."(John 13 v 26) They were all so preoccupied with their own thoughts that nobody seemed to notice that this man was Judas Iscariot. Jesus said quietly to him, "What you are about to do, do quickly." (John 13 v 27)

When the betrayer had left, Jesus took bread, broke it and passed it on to his disciples. "This is my body given for you. Do this in remembrance of me." (Luke 22 v 19) The disciples looked completely unperturbed as they ate the bread. Then Jesus took the cup, saying, "This cup is the new covenant in my blood, which is poured out for you." (Luke 22 v 20) They each drank, but most of them had confused or glazed looks in their eyes.

When they had finished the meal, Jesus looked fondly at each of the eleven in turn before saying, "Let us praise God in song and prayer."

In this, his last Passover meal on earth, Jesus demonstrated his deep love and compassion for all his disciples and, indeed, for all mankind.

Raphael
The Heavenly Chronicle

It was especially uplifting for Raphael to watch the Son of God sharing a special moment of worship with his disciples before going out and willingly subjecting himself to the horrendous suffering that lay before him – as foretold by the prophets. But although Raphael's heart was being stirred by the beauty of the intimate praise and worship he was witnessing, he was anxious to see what the betrayer was doing at that very moment. So he left the room, searched the area below him and noticed that Judas was hurrying towards the temple.

When the betrayer had reached the temple, Raphael was concerned to see Judas pushing himself forward, so determined was he to see the high priests in their inner sanctum. Until he remembered some prophecies: from Zechariah, "I told them, 'if you think it best, give me my pay; but if not, keep it.' So they paid me thirty pieces of silver. And the Lord said to me, 'Throw it to the potter' – the handsome price at which they priced me!' So I took the thirty pieces of silver and threw them into the house of the Lord to the potter." (Zechariah 11 vs 12–13) And from the Psalms: " Even my close friend, whom I trusted, he who shared my bread, has lifted up his heel against me." (Psalm 41 v 9) Of course: this was the betrayer at work, Judas Iscariot who was deliberately choosing to turn against his Lord and Master. Judas Iscariot who, like so many of the other Jews, wanted a warrior king who would use his might and his power to conquer the Romans and free them all from their subjugation to this hated occupier. Why should they pay extortionate taxes to a foreign ruler thousands of stadia away? And why shouldn't they elect a leader who was prepared to go into battle and defeat the Romans!

Raphael had heard Judas talking to other groups of men, men he later learnt were known as the Zealots. He knew very well that Judas had never really approved of Jesus' methods. And now this foolish man was acting on his dissatisfaction. You would think after all those months of sitting under Jesus' teaching and being in such close proximity with him for three whole years, not to mention all the spectacular miracles he had witnessed, he would have realised who it was he was intending to betray. Or hadn't he listened to anything Jesus had said or watched anything he had done! How shocking that this man was about to betray his Master for such a paltry sum of money – the cheapest price fetched for any slave. How terrible that he was prepared to betray his compassionate, loving Master at all. But it was written. The prophets had foretold it thousands of years ago. And now it was being enacted before Raphael's very eyes.

So Raphael watched Judas approach the high priests, he listened to him crudely haggling over the price of the betrayal, he heard him agreeing to the very price the prophets had foretold: thirty pieces of silver. What an insult to God. What a disgrace.

Raphael turned his face away after noticing the triumphant smirk on the betrayer's face. His heart was very heavy as he winged his way back to his Master. As he flew back to Jesus and his disciples, he was mindful of the prophecies about the suffering of the Messiah, particularly those in the Psalms and Isaiah. Psalm 22 presented a graphic prophecy of the Christ's agony:

"I am poured out like water, and all my bones are out of joint.

My heart has turned to wax;

it has melted away within me.

My strength is dried up like a potsherd,

and my tongue sticks to the roof of my mouth;

you lay me in the dust of death.

Dogs have surrounded me;

a band of evil men has encircled me,

they have pierced my hands and my feet.

I can count all my bones;

people stare and gloat over me.

They divide my garments among them and cast lots for my clothing. " (Psalm 22 vs 14–18)

Raphael shuddered as he pictured the torment and agony the King of the universe was about to endure. He was utterly amazed that anyone, least of all the King of glory, could offer himself up as a willing sacrifice for sinful man. Yet that is what Jesus was doing as he resolutely walked with his disciples towards the Mount of Olives. As soon as he arrived in the Garden of Gethsemane, Jesus told his disciples to watch and pray, while he went deeper into the garden, dropped to his knees and began an agonised prayer to his Father.

While all this was going on, Raphael was distressed to observe that Jesus' disciples were sleeping nearby. Couldn't they stay awake at this critical time in their teacher's life, even after he had expressly instructed them to "Watch and pray, that you do not fall into temptation."

Chapter Twenty-Seven

This was a very sombre time for Raphael. He couldn't bring himself to write about the Messiah's foretold suffering. In any case, he sensed the presence of many hovering angels, and he imagined that heaven was waiting breathlessly for the fulfilment of God's plan on earth.

So, with a greatly saddened heart, he watched the Lord sweating blood. Not only was he experiencing physical suffering as he struggled with the full knowledge of what was about to transpire; but he was also feeling such intense mental anguish as he grappled in prayer with his Father. His movements were restless: his whole body shook as he raised his arms to the heavens, pleading with his Father. Although Raphael could empathise deeply with the Christ, he was well aware that he couldn't possibly know or even understand the full extent of his Lord and Master's suffering. He could sense the presence of that evil fallen angel, the devil, maliciously and desperately tempting Jesus – his Lord and Master flung his arms to one side, as if trying to swat off the presence of the tempter. Then, in a broken voice which seemed to Raphael to contain all the suffering in the world, Jesus pleaded with his father to take the cup of suffering away from him. Yet even as he was experiencing this dire mental agony, he cried out, "Yet not my will, but yours be done." (Luke 22 v 42)

Raphael felt the air all around him being disturbed by a sudden rush of wind. He jerked his head up, expecting to be disturbed by some evil force. But to his great relief, he saw one of his colleagues from the heavenly realms, winging his way towards them. He flew straight to Jesus, and without saying anything, he slowly and lovingly wiped a cloth across his face. After he had finished, his hands slid to Jesus' shoulders where they remained. Raphael could see, already, that the comfort from the angel was having a positive effect on Jesus. His prostrate body began to straighten up: he pushed back his shoulders and raised his chin, a resolute expression in his eyes.

When the angel left him, Raphael thought he heard a slow, mournful dirge filtering down to him from the heavens: a painfully slow drumbeat, low notes of a bassoon and the mournful sounds of the oboe.

But when the betrayer approached with a crowd of men armed with clubs and swords, even that mournful music came to an abrupt halt. It was as if the angels were already mourning for the Son of God as he deliberately set his face towards the painful, agonising road towards his death. The moment that Jesus got up and said to his closest disciples, "The hour has come. Look, the Son of Man is betrayed into the hands of sinners" (Mark 14 v 41), the atmosphere was fraught with tension. Especially as the crowd Judas was leading into the garden was armed with clubs and swords. This gave Jesus a reason to comment on his peaceful mission. "Am I leading a rebellion," he said, "that you have come with swords and clubs? Every day I was with you in the temple courts, and you did not lay a hand on me. But this is your hour – when darkness reigns.:(Luke 22, vs 52-53)

The rowdy crowd didn't appear to be listening. Clearly, they wanted to see some action that night: a thrilling arrest, a man being led off in ropes, a trial at the house of the high priest. And the man they had come to arrest was a great catch: a man everyone was accusing of blasphemy, the worst sin you could possibly commit against the holy God of the heavens. When Judas walked towards Jesus, some of the men were jostling each other for a good position at the front; they wanted to be the first to see the blasphemer tied up and dragged in front of the high priest and his councillors to answer for his crimes.

Raphael was incredibly saddened as Judas, pretending to be friendly and 'loving', went right up to Jesus and gave him a kiss. Jesus cried out, "Judas, are you betraying the Son of Man with a kiss?" (Luke 22 v 48)

The men who had come to arrest Jesus used unnecessary force against him now, because Jesus handed himself over to them like a lamb: they grabbed his wrists, pulling the rope tightly around them to make sure he was trussed up like a common criminal. They shoved him from behind whilst someone grabbed his robe and pulled him from the front. But Jesus held his head high and willingly subjected himself to their indignities and insults. And even in this dire situation, the Son of Man found the time to heal one of his attackers. Raphael was horrified when he saw Peter drawing a sword and thrusting it violently at one of the soldiers, cutting off his ear. Instead of encouraging his followers to defend him or commending Peter for his action, Jesus rebuked his disciple and used his power to heal the afflicted man's ear.

As Raphael observed the callous actions of these arrogant, puny men, he felt like crying out in a loud voice, "Do you realise whom you are insulting?" He was finding it very difficult to be restrained, and did wish, for a moment, that he could be more distant from this event and from what was about to happen. But that was a cowardly response. He knew he had to watch and wait as Jesus fulfilled the plan of God by sacrificing himself for the sins of the world.

What Raphael found most disturbing of all as Jesus was pushed and jostled through the streets, the jeering crowds insulting and abusing him, was the speed at which all his followers deserted him. At least Peter was trailing behind at a distance. But judging by what Jesus had said to him, this could only end badly. When challenged, Peter would desert Jesus too.

What followed next was very hard to watch: Peter's desertion of Jesus, false witness after false witness accusing Jesus with anything they could think of, the high priest badgering him to answer the many accusations against him. But Jesus remained silent. Even when yet another malicious witness came forward and quoted him as saying, "I am willing to destroy this temple of God and rebuild it again in three days, he didn't even try to correct him. He could have so easily explained that he wasn't talking about the temple, but about his earthly body. However, the time for explanations and teaching was finished; in its place had come the time of suffering.

Jesus' silence was making the high priest more and more frustrated. Finally, he challenged Jesus directly, saying, "Tell us, under oath, are you the Christ, the Son of God?"

"Yes, it is as you say. But I say to all of you: In the future you will see the Son of Man sitting at the right hand of the Mighty One and coming on the clouds of heaven." (Matthew 26 v 64)The high priest was absolutely furious. He tore his clothes and boomed, "Why do we need any more witnesses? We have heard the blasphemy from his own lips."

Someone else said, "He is worthy of death." (Matthew 26 v 66)

Raphael could hardly bear to look as the abuse of his Lord and Master intensified. They spat in his face, blindfolded him and struck him with their fists. " Prophecy to us, Christ, who hit you?"

After some time, Caiaphas pronounced in a business-like fashion, "He needs to be taken before the governor. It is important that Pontius Pilate gets to understand the seriousness of the heinous crime of blasphemy this man has committed against our God and against our nation."

So a large crowd went with Jesus to the governor's residence. But they did not go inside, as they did not want to pollute themselves by entering the place of a pagan Roman governor before the Sabbath day. So Pilate came out to them. After listening to the many accusations the chief priest and his councillors levelled against Jesus, he addressed him directly: "Are you the king of the Jews?"

Once again, Jesus replied with the simple truth, "Yes, it is as you say."

Then the chief priests and elders were shouting their accusations at Jesus so loudly that Pilate decided to take him inside for a private audience. There, he asked Jesus more about his claim to be the king of the Jews. He seemed very puzzled by his answer, "My kingdom is not of this world. If it were, my servants would fight to prevent my arrest by the Jews. But now my kingdom is from another place." (John 18 v 36)

Pilate seemed puzzled. He didn't seem to know what to say to Jesus, especially after their discussion about what truth was. So he got up abruptly, taking Jesus outside to his accusers. "I find no basis for a charge against this man," (Luke 23 v 4) he said.

"He's a Galilean and he is subverting our nation," they cried.

"Aaah! A Galilean!" replied Pilate. "He must go to Herod then. The king of his district should try him."

Even though Raphael knew about the dire prophecies relating to Jesus' suffering, the actual events unfolding beneath him appeared to be so much worse. To witness the Christ in the raw flesh being violently assaulted, spat at and scorned, was almost unendurable. But for Jesus, the mental and spiritual torment must have been so much more severe. Was he wondering where his father was while he was suffering so much; or was he encouraged by the fact that – despite what mere men said – he was indeed his son. And that when his torment was over, and he had completed the work the father had given him to do, he would indeed be sitting at the right hand of his father in heaven? And what restraint to know that he could call upon his father to send legions of angels to rescue him – yet not to do it. His motivation? He knew it was not the will of his father. Jesus' total obedience to his father, his endurance, calmness and resoluteness to do only his father's will, were all an incredible encouragement to Raphael. What an awe-inspiring example his Master was to himself, the other angels and to the whole of humankind.

Jesus was unceremoniously dragged, pushed and shoved through the streets all the way to Herod's palace. Herod couldn't contain his delight when Jesus was brought before him and he heard all the accusations the high priest and other religious leaders levelled against him.

Rubbing his hands together, he said, "Aaah, the wonder-worker. I've heard a lot about you."

Jesus was silent.

"You are the man who can perform magic tricks," he said sarcastically.

Jesus remained silent. This made Herod very angry. "Guards," he ordered, "get this insolent prisoner to talk."

Two burly guards went straight up to Jesus. One punched him on the jaw while the other spat in his face.

"Now," said Herod, addressing Jesus, "my soldiers know very well how to deliver a sound beating. But I am a magnanimous king. And I am known for enjoying my entertainment – first-class entertainment. So, if you perform some magic tricks for me… but make sure they are spectacular… I might even find it in my heart to let you go."

Herod waited.

But Jesus stood there as silently as a lamb before the slaughter.

Suddenly, Herod lost interest. With a dismissive gesture of his hands, he said to his guards, "Teach this prisoner a lesson for wasting my time. Give him a sound beating and send him back to Pilate. And thank Pilate for his 'gift' of this unresponsive criminal, but tell him that he is of no use to me."

"But he's from Galilee… "

"What's that to me?" said Herod angrily, rising and clapping his hands. "Pilate can deal with him. Bring me my wine and my women."

Once again, Raphael turned his face away because he couldn't bear to watch the torture the king of the universe was being subjected to, nor could he face watching his arduous journey back to Pilate, the abusive crowd doing anything they could to humiliate the king of the Jews.

The crowds spat, shouted and hurled insults at Jesus as he was being taken back to Pilates' residence. Even as Jesus was approaching, Raphael noticed a flurry of movement at the governor's quarters. Pilate had gone onto the paved exterior of his palatial dwelling and was standing between two pillars watching all the activity surrounding the return of the prisoner. A group of women headed by a beautiful lady in a flowing white robe, her long black hair all awry, rushed up to him. The woman, who was obviously his wife, clasped his arm and said, "Don't have anything to do with that innocent prisoner."

Instead of answering her directly, Pilate said, "I see Herod has sent him back to me. So it seems I will be the one who has to decide his fate."

At this, his wife looked even more distraught. "I have had a very bad dream. An omen from the gods. I am pleading with you, don't touch this case. That man is innocent."

He replied almost absent-mindedly, "We will see. We will see. Now go inside with your ladies. The rabble is almost upon us."

Casting a pained look over her shoulder, she retreated, but before she went inside, she turned around and called, "Don't spill the blood of an innocent man."

The crowd surged forward, but stopped at the steps leading up to the paved area where Pilate was standing. The high priest led Jesus to Pilate, who was obviously in deep thought. His chin was resting in his cupped hand and he had a serious expression on his face. He turned to the crowd, the sombre expression lifting from his face.

"As is the custom at the time of the Passover feast, I can release one prisoner to you. Which one do you want me to release to you: Barabbas, or Jesus who is called the Christ?" (Matthew 27 v 17)

But the crowd were baying for Jesus' blood. "Crucify him, crucify him," (Matthew 27 v 22)they shouted.

"Why, what crime has he committed?" (Matthew 17 v 23)

"Blasphemy," boomed the high priest, "a crime worthy of death. And he claims to be a king. Caesar would not be pleased."

"Try him by your own laws."

"But we cannot give the death penalty. That is why you must judge him for his serious crimes."

"Very well then, I will have him punished," he said with authority. "Guards, take him away for the thirty lashes." Abruptly, Pilate left them while Jesus was dragged to a large courtyard with an ominous-looking whipping post. He was stripped of his clothes and manacled to the post.

Not for the first time that day, Raphael turned his head away. But even though he wasn't looking, he could hear the savage whips whistling through the air and ripping the Son of God's flesh apart, over and over again. A large crowd of soldiers had gathered to watch the punishment – Raphael also heard their jeering cries. This atrocious assault on the innocent flesh of his Lord and Master seemed to last indefinitely. But what Raphael didn't hear was a single cry from his Master's lips. Throughout this savage attack on his flesh, Jesus was silent. At last the whips stopped and Jesus was set free from the post.

But his torture wasn't over. The soldiers seemed to be just warming up to their sadistic task. To his horror, Raphael saw that a soldier had twisted together a crown of thorns. Another was carrying a purple robe and a 'sceptre'. Someone else brought a chair. When they had forced the purple robe onto Jesus, they shoved him into his seat and placed a sceptre in one of his hands. "A king must have a crown," said the soldier who was carrying the crown of thorns. "Oh king, we need to borrow your royal sceptre." Wrenching it from his hand, he placed the crown of thorns on Jesus' head and began hammering it down into Jesus' flesh. The agony must have been unendurable, but Jesus managed to remain silent.

Some of the soldiers knelt before him and cried out, "O king, O king." Others spat in his face. "Shall we take you to the governor now," said one soldier. "Perhaps you and he can make a decree together."

"Better put him in his own garments now." This was followed by raucous laughter. A muscular soldier had to rip off Jesus' purple robe which had stuck to his wounds. Some of his skin must have been mixed with the blood of his raw wounds. The pain must have been extremely severe. The same soldier thrust Jesus' own garment over his head and another soldier dragged him, stumbling, towards Pilate. He pushed him in front of the governor.

Pilate gestured to Jesus and said, "Here is your king."(John 19 v 14)

"We have no king but Caesar," screamed the crowd.

Pilate turned to a soldier. "Bring out Barabbas."

A burly, chained man was pushed to the paved area. On the one side of him, Pilate presented Jesus, who was barely able to stand; on the other side, Barabbas, a murderer who had taken part in the insurrection. Pilate addressed the crowd: "Whom shall I release to you: Barabbas, or Jesus of Nazareth?"

"Barabbas, release Barabbas," they chanted. "We want Barabbas."

"What shall I do, then, with Jesus of Nazareth?"

"Crucify him, crucify him." Their chanting became louder and louder and louder – so loud that Raphael flew a little higher to get away from their vicious, vindictive chant.

"Bring me a bowl of water," Pilate cried to one of his attendants.

When it arrived, he immediately made a public display of thoroughly washing his hands. "See," he cried out in a loud voice, "I have no part in this. Take him to the people."

Raphael couldn't believe his ears when he heard the people actually cheering as soon as Pilate announced this. Someone had already brought a large wooden cross which they shoved onto Jesus' shoulders. "See if you can carry that... you're such a powerful king."

Jesus stumbled and staggered forward, the heavy weight of the cross bearing down on his broken body.

Raphael, his senses keenly attuned to what was going on around him, once again thought he heard the soft strains of a mournful dirge in the heavens above. He also felt the presence of unseen angelic beings hovering in the air. A deep humming sound encircled him and his arms were showered with what felt like steady rain. But when he looked up at the cloudless sky, he realised that the drops of water he had felt were angels' tears.

The dirge and the humming continued all the way to the hill called Calvary. On the way, Raphael had also seen many women weeping copious tears. But the biggest ordeal for his beloved Master was yet to come. Extremely weak and bleeding profusely from his many wounds, including the ripped flesh around his face and skull from that cruel 'crown' of thorns, the soldiers stretched Jesus out on that large wooden cross. And instead of tying his hands and feet as they did with many other criminals, they took four large nails and hammered them into his hands and his feet. Raphael couldn't even begin to imagine how excruciatingly painful that must have been. With every blow that was delivered to the King of the universe, he found himself cringing, as if his own celestial body was being assaulted. As Jesus' cross was raised, the sky darkened and a dim black night descended onto the earth. The celestial dirge began again, but now it was accompanied by the wailing of the earthly women who stood some distance from the cross. Mary, Jesus' mother, however, supported by Mary

Magdalene, stood at the foot of the cross, weeping, as the soldiers divided Jesus' clothes amongst themselves and cast lots for his seamless garment.

But even in his direst agony at the hands of these brutal soldiers, Jesus extended grace to his torturers. "Father," he said, "forgive them, for they do not know what they are doing." (Luke 23 v 34)

Meanwhile the chief priests, elders and other men of authority seemed to find sadistic pleasure in taunting Jesus over and over again, and in hurling insults at him.

"He saved others, but he can't even save himself!"

"But he's supposed to be a king! And a powerful one at that."

"Let him prove he's a king."

"Yes. See if he can come down from the cross. Then we can believe in him!"

"He said he was God's son. So let God rescue him now if he wants him so much."

Raphael was so upset with these insolent, arrogant mortals. How dare they heap insult after insult on their very Maker! But Raphael saw that it wasn't only influential men who were mocking his Lord. Jesus was flanked by two criminals, one on his right and the other on his left. One of them began to insult Jesus: "Some king of the Jews! If you really were as great as people say, you'd save us and yourself."

"Stop pestering him," said the other man. "He's done nothing wrong, but we are being justly punished." Then, turning to Jesus, he said, "Remember me when you come into your kingdom."

"I tell you the truth, today you will be with me in paradise." (Luke 23 vs 42- 43) Raphael was touched that his Master, even in his great agony, could be so compassionate towards a sinful man. And even as he hung there, dying, Jesus showed great compassion for his mother who was weeping below him as John tried to comfort her. "Dear woman," he said to Mary, "here is your son." And to John: "Here is your mother." (John 19 v 26)

John allowed her head to drop onto his shoulder as she continued to weep profusely. He steadied her, putting a supporting arm around her waist. What torment for a mother to see her very special son suffer so intensely – and to be unable to do anything about it. The burden on her soul must be almost too much to bear.

The darkness seemed to intensify as Jesus cried out in a loud voice, "My God, my God, why have you forsaken me?" (Matthew 27 v 46)

How could his father look on when Jesus, at that moment, was stained by the sins of the whole world. What a heavy burden to carry. And how lonely and isolated Jesus was. No-one, not the angels, not even his beloved father, was there to comfort him in his extreme suffering.

"I am thirsty," (John 19 v 28) Jesus gasped. Raphael saw a soldier dipping a sponge into some wine vinegar, placing the sponge onto the end of a long, sharp stick, and pushing it up to Jesus' lips. But Jesus turned his face aside; he did not drink.

"Now leave him alone," taunted the soldier. Let's see if Elijah comes to save him."

In the blackness, the tension was building up. Finally, Jesus called out in a loud voice, "It is finished."(John 19 v 30)

247

Then, crying out again in a loud voice, "Father, into your hands I commit my spirit," (Luke 23 v 46) he gave up his spirit. At last, his suffering was over! A little while later, two soldiers came with hammers to break the legs of the criminals.

"Hey," said one soldier, "this guy's already dead so we don't have to break his bones."

"Let's be quite sure," replied his companion, thrusting his spear into Jesus' side. "Dead all right," he pronounced, as a mixture of blood and water flowed onto the ground.

At that moment, the earth shook, the rocks splitting from the violent earthquake. The centurion who was guarding the bodies crouched down and put his arm over his face in sheer terror.

"Surely he was the Son of God," (Matthew 27 v 54) he cried out. Raphael could hear a deep humming sound from above his head, starting softly and then reaching a crescendo. No tuning of violins now; not even the more sombre instruments were being used and there were certainly no joyful choruses of 'Hallelujas'. Instead, there was this continuous, lamenting moan from the angels who were clearly in deep mourning.

Although it was still dark, Raphael could see people stirring at the back of the crowd. A man in priestly robes was running forward, in search of the high priest. "Caiaphas, Caiaphas," he shouted urgently, "something terrible has happened in the temple."

Caiaphas left the priests who were clustered near the cross and hurried to meet the man. "What is it? What has happened?"

"The curtain in front of the most holy place has torn in two, from top to bottom."

"Sacrilege – worse than blasphemy," cried Caiaphas, tearing his robes. "Who is responsible for this dastardly act?"

"That's the thing… I… was there… Nobody went near the curtain. It just tore by itself – like it was ripped in two with an unseen hand."

"Preposterous! I'm going there to investigate right now."

But Raphael, for the first time since Jesus had been arrested in the garden, had a broad smile on his face. Free access to God for men? With no intermediary! Surely that was what the ripped curtain signified. What a powerful symbol. And this had all been made possible by the Son of God's death on the cross. A perfect sacrifice for the sins of the people. What a magnificent exchange. Achieved at great expense to himself, Jesus Christ, at his death, had willingly suffered so that he could become the saviour of the world. All the people had to do was repent and turn to him.

Caiaphas was so flustered by the 'bad news' he had heard about the tearing of the curtain in front of the holy place that he cried out, "The torn curtain – before the most holy place – what a disaster." So, accompanied by the other priest and members of the Council, he hurried from Calvary to try to sort out what he perceived to be a serious problem at the temple.

Raphael saw another prominent man walking towards the cross and approaching the chief guard, showing him a scroll. "I am Joseph of Arimathea. The governor has given me permission to take this body and bury it." The guard shrugged, and when Jesus' body was taken down from the cross, after Mary had mourned over it, he allowed Joseph to cover it in a clean linen cloth. Raphael followed Joseph as he took the body away from Calvary, that place of agony and endurance; he saw Joseph placing Jesus' body in a brand new garden tomb. There he laid Jesus' body. Raphael decided to watch and wait. So when three particularly burly soldiers arrived at the tomb, he was a little concerned that they might do some damage to Jesus' body. One of them spoke to the guard on duty: "We have orders to seal this tomb."

"What for?" replied the guard.

"Fanatical Jewish leaders! Worried that this man's disciples might steal him away and tell everyone he's risen from the dead."

"You're not serious?"

"Dead serious!"

The soldier laughed.

"Now come on, help us. We've got to roll this huge stone across the entrance and seal it. And just in case you think you're getting some time off, we've all been ordered to guard the tomb – all night and all day – until the first day of the week has passed."

"You're joking! That seems a bit excessive doesn't it – for a common criminal."

"Well there's all this king of the Jews stuff… and that crazy dead man said he was going to rise from the dead after three days."

"Soft in the head."

"Maybe, but the authorities are taking this very seriously. They don't want his followers stealing the body and then spreading rumours and telling lies… so let's get to it. They'll be after us if we don't do this properly."

The soldier just stood there, gaping.

"Hurry up. Help us push," was the sharp command.

"How futile," thought Raphael. " Who could contain the Son of God? These were soldiers who had been taught the art of war, but what about the Jewish authorities who should know better? How could those who had diligently studied the scriptures possibly miss the many prophecies from the Psalms and the prophets pointing to Jesus' death and resurrection? At the forefront of Raphael's mind were two scriptures in particular, but there were many others. What did the high priests and elders make of Hosea's words, "After two days he will revive us; on the third day he will restore us, that we may live in his presence." (Hosea 6 v 2)

Were they blind? And deaf? Or were they so involved in their own sinful pursuits that they had lost the gift of being able to interpret the scriptures correctly?

On the Sabbath day itself, things were very quiet at the tomb. The soldiers guarded it diligently, but nobody came near it that day. In keeping with the Sabbath laws, all the Jewish people who considered themselves to be orthodox were worshipping and doing no work. The spices for Jesus' body that had been prepared the day before would be brought by the women the next day to embalm the body of their Lord. Raphael, also, kept watch, conscious of the distant mournful humming that filled the heavens. During that time of quiet meditation, he praised and honoured the son for all the work he had done on earth, and was continuing to do by his sacrificial death.

But as the foretold triumphal day got closer, the mournful dirge was replaced by what Raphael could only describe as 'shimmering' music: the tone was soft and very sweet – not a full melody, yet it sounded as if multitudes of harpists were lightly plucking their strings over and over again. Almost as if these angelic musicians were waiting for something glorious to happen; they were marking their time until they could join with the complete heavenly orchestra and the full participation of all the celestial choirs – whose mission it would be to praise and honour and glorify the suffering servant who was King of Kings and Lord of Lords.

When the first day of the week did finally arrive, very early in the morning, the ground suddenly began to shake so much that even the extremely heavy stone in front of the tomb was rolled away. The guards were so terrified that they became like statuettes, frozen to the ground. Raphael noticed a white-hot light seeping from the tomb, then there was a sudden rush of air as Jesus, in all his glory and splendour, his arms raised up to heaven, shot up like lightning into the sky, leaving a trail of golden light behind him.

Raphael couldn't restrain himself. Instead of getting out his stylus to write an article, he flew straight up to heaven, shouting in a loud voice, " Hallelujah, he is risen. " The angel choirs took up this refrain, and soon the whole of heaven was filled with the triumphant news of the Christ's resurrection from the dead. Exultantly, Raphael took his place in the heavenly throng, praising God for raising his son from the dead and glorifying Jesus for his sacrificial work on earth. Now that it was finished, all of mankind had been shown the way to the Father. They just had to believe in the Son of God, repent, and come to him; for he had saved them from the coming judgement.

Raphael received such a warm-hearted welcome in heaven that in an instant, it felt as if he had never been away. How good it was to be home. The richness of the melodies and harmonies that surrounded him filled Raphael's spirit with a deep sense of thanksgiving. It was wonderful to be back again in heaven, where the praise was unending; what a privilege it was to be able to concentrate entirely on worshipping God the Father and his Son, Jesus Christ.

And although during the next forty days, Jesus still had to make brief visits to the earth to prove to his followers that he was alive, to inspire them and to help them to set up his church on the earth, the assurance of his constant presence with them for all eternity thrilled Raphael's heart. Because there truly was no-one like Jesus, the unique Son of God who had offered his life as a ransom for many.

Raphael felt so privileged that he had been included, albeit in a very small way, in God's ultimate plan to glorify his Son and to install him as the judge of the whole world.